DC COMICS™
SUPER HEROES

GREEN LANTERN™

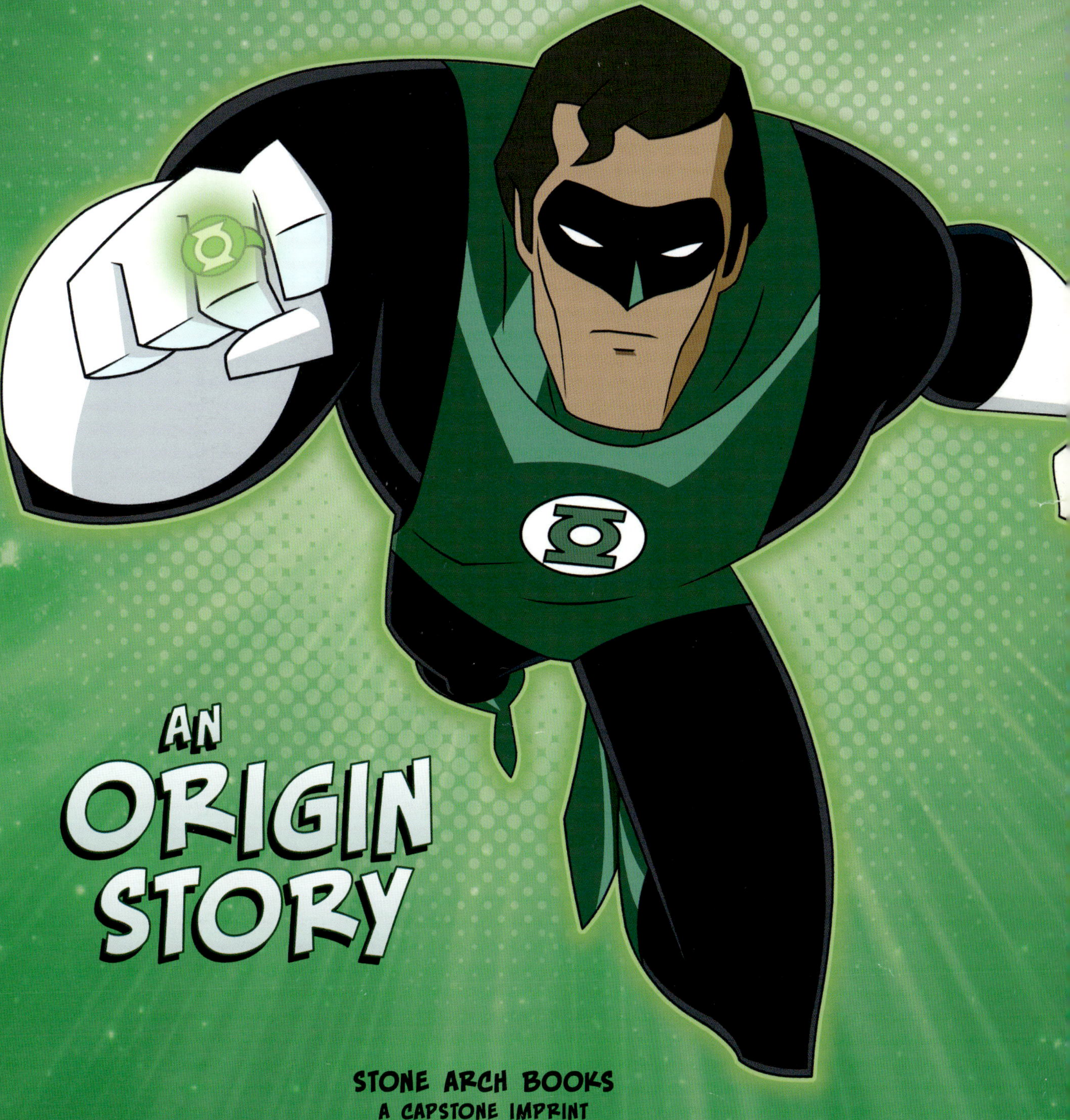

AN ORIGIN STORY

STONE ARCH BOOKS
A CAPSTONE IMPRINT

Published by Stone Arch Books in 2015
A Capstone Imprint
1710 Roe Crest Drive
North Mankato, MN 56003
www.capstonepub.com

STAR34385

Cataloging-in-Publication Data is available at the Library of Congress website
ISBN: 978-1-4342-9730-3 (library binding)
ISBN: 978-1-4342-9734-1 (paperback)
ISBN: 978-1-4965-0164-6 (eBook)

Summary: In brightest day and in blackest night, Hal Jordan heeds all calls for help as sector 2814's
Green Lantern. But before Hal became a galactic guardian, he was a test pilot for the U.S. Air
Force. Follow in Hal's footsteps as he becomes the greatest Green Lantern of all! This action-packed
chapter book for early readers is filled with comic art by DC Comics illustrators.

Contributing artists: Dan Schoening, Erik Doescher,
Mike DeCarlo, Lee Loughridge
Designed by Hilary Wacholz

Printed in the United States of America in North Mankato, Minnesota
092014   008482CGS15

DC COMICS™
SUPER HEROES

Green Lantern

AN ORIGIN STORY

WRITTEN BY
MATTHEW K. MANNING

ILLUSTRATED BY
LUCIANO VECCHIO

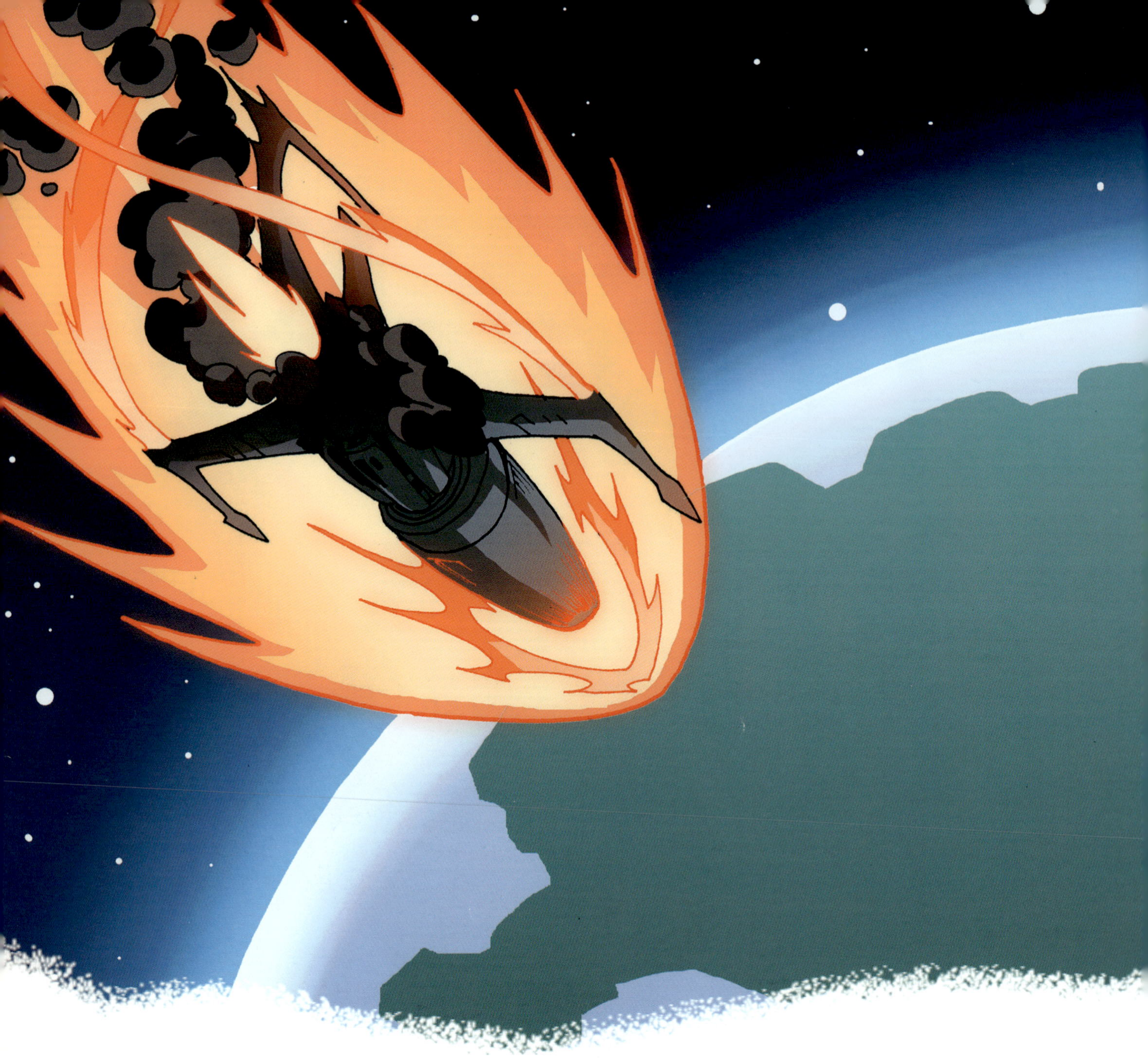

Everything is quiet. A ship plummets toward Earth. No one can hear the whine of the ship's engines. There is no sound in space.

But inside the craft, things are different. The whir of computer parts is loud. The emergency alarms are deafening.

This alien is named Abin Sur. He comes from a world far away from our own.

He is a champion in that place. But his time is almost at its end . . .

"Ring," Abin Sur says. "Find my replacement. Find a man on this world . . . a man who knows no fear. Find the next Green Lantern."

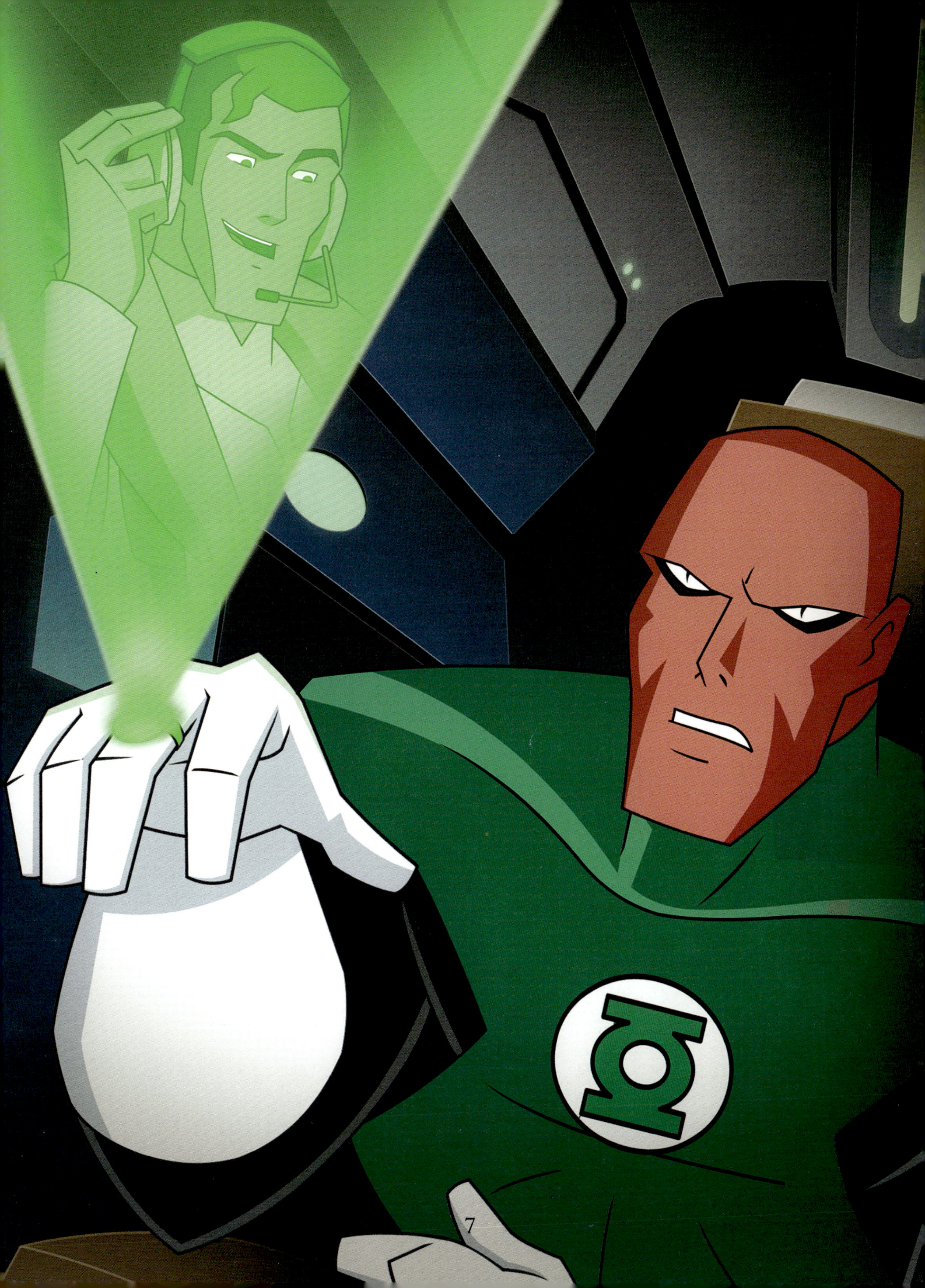

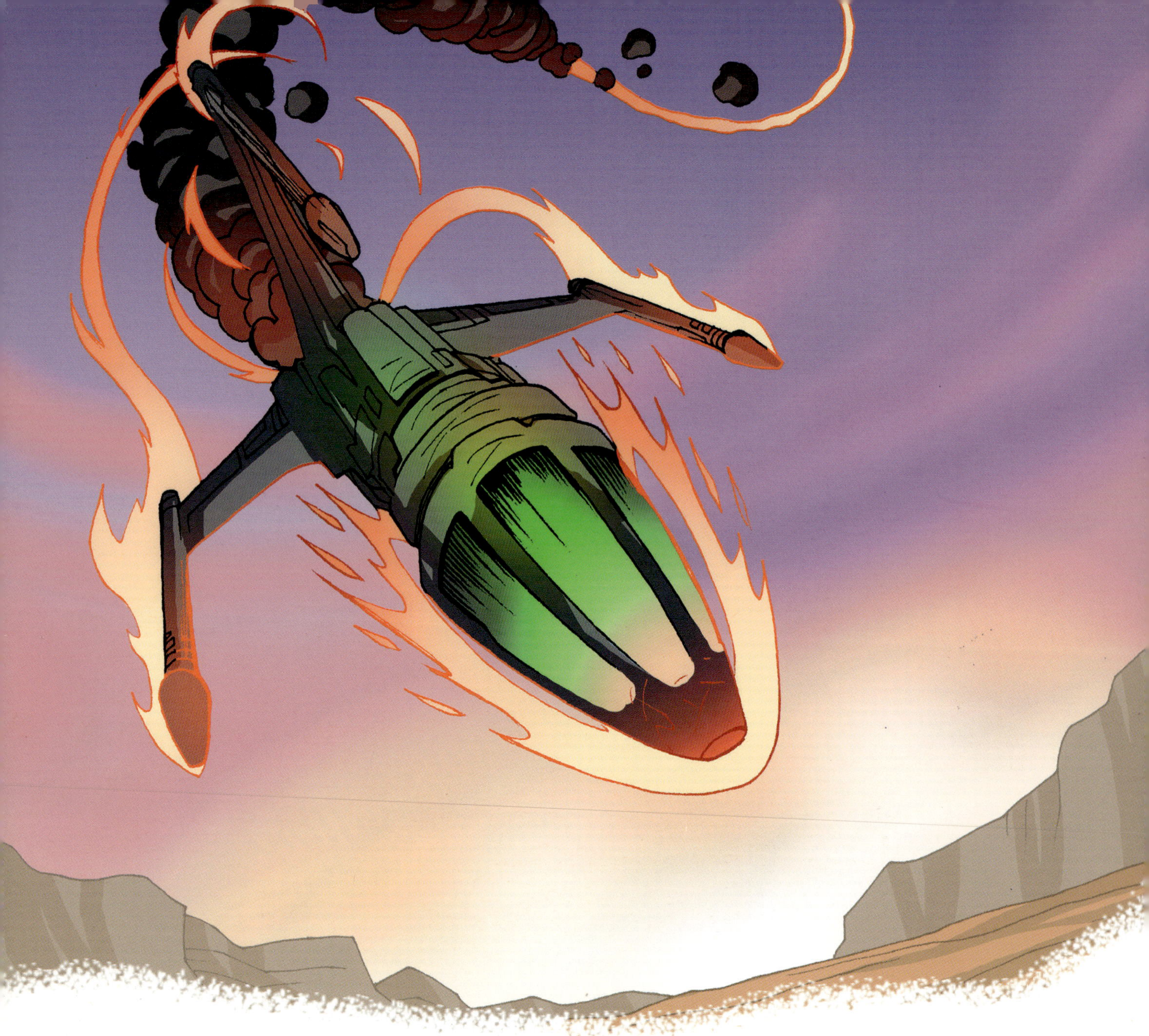

The ring's answer can't be heard over the roaring flames. The ship is no longer in outer space. It has entered Earth's atmosphere.

There is nothing quiet about this man or his plane. His name is Hal Jordan. Flying is what he does best.

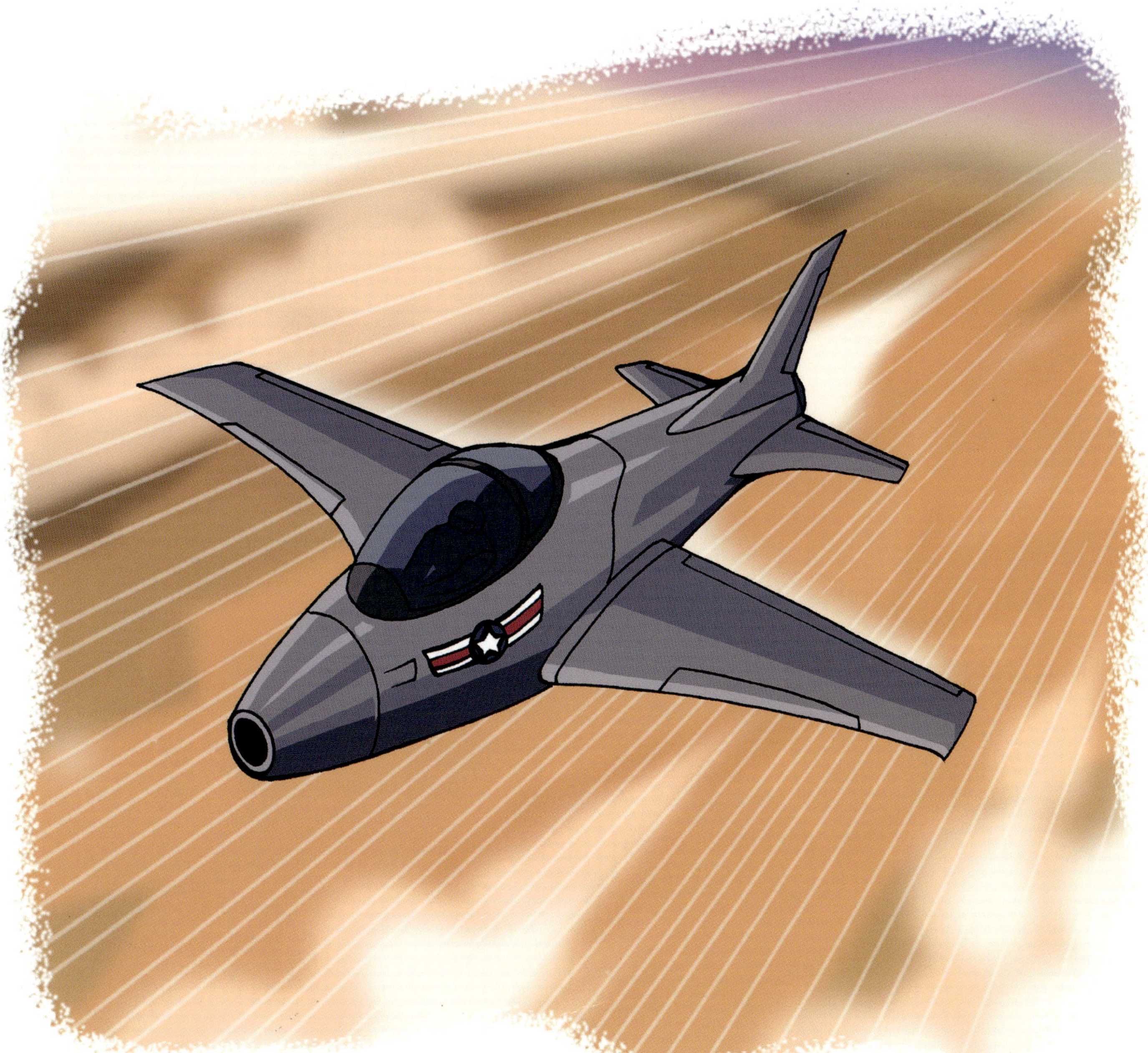

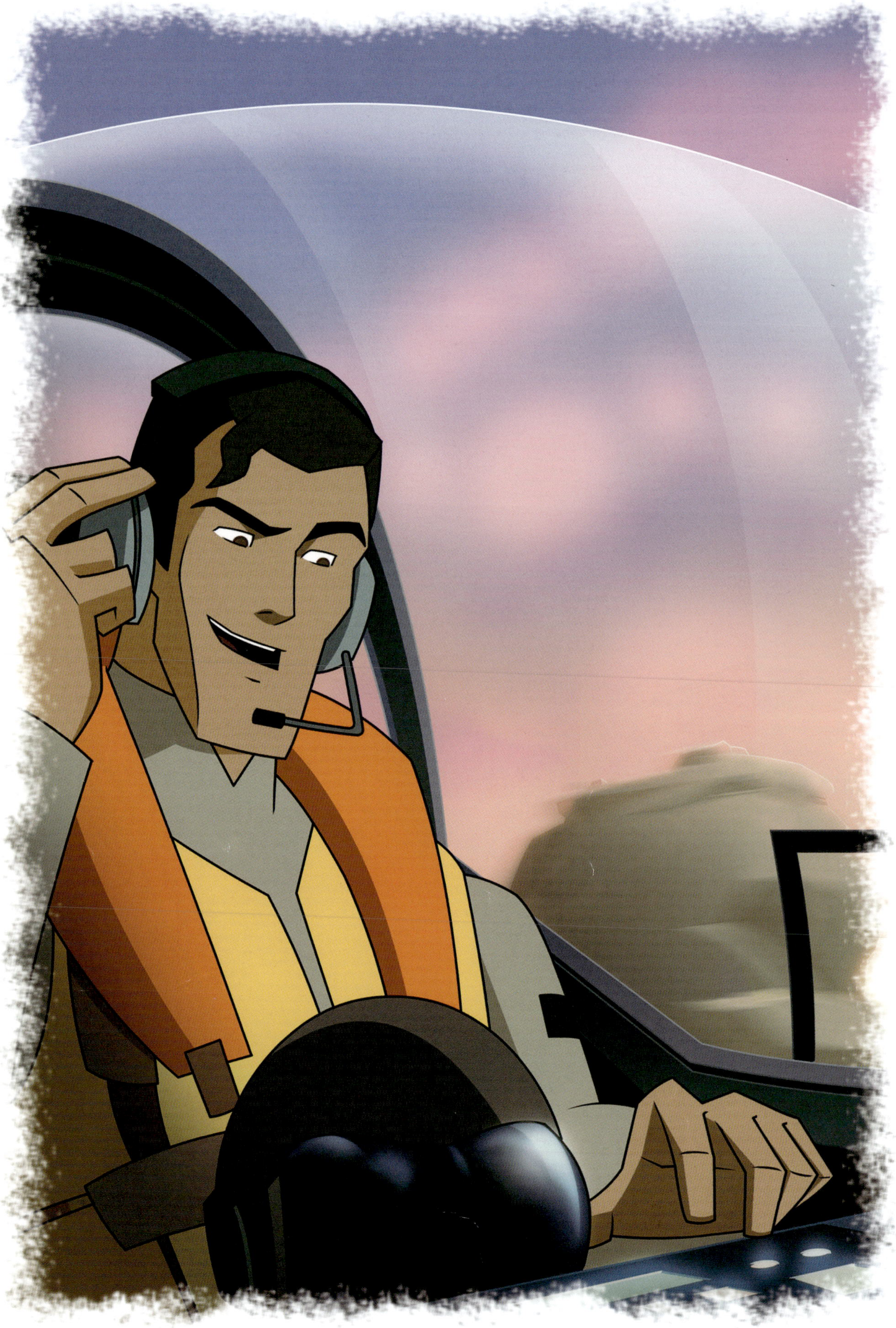

"You're taking it too high," someone says through Hal's headset. The voice belongs to Carol Ferris, Hal's boss.

He should really listen to her. But he doesn't. Instead, Hal takes the plane higher.

"I'm a test pilot, Carol," Hal says. "I'm going to do my job. Let's see what this thing can do!"

The jet continues to climb. Just then, the engines shut off. "Wait," Hal says. He looks down at his controls. There's no noise coming from them.

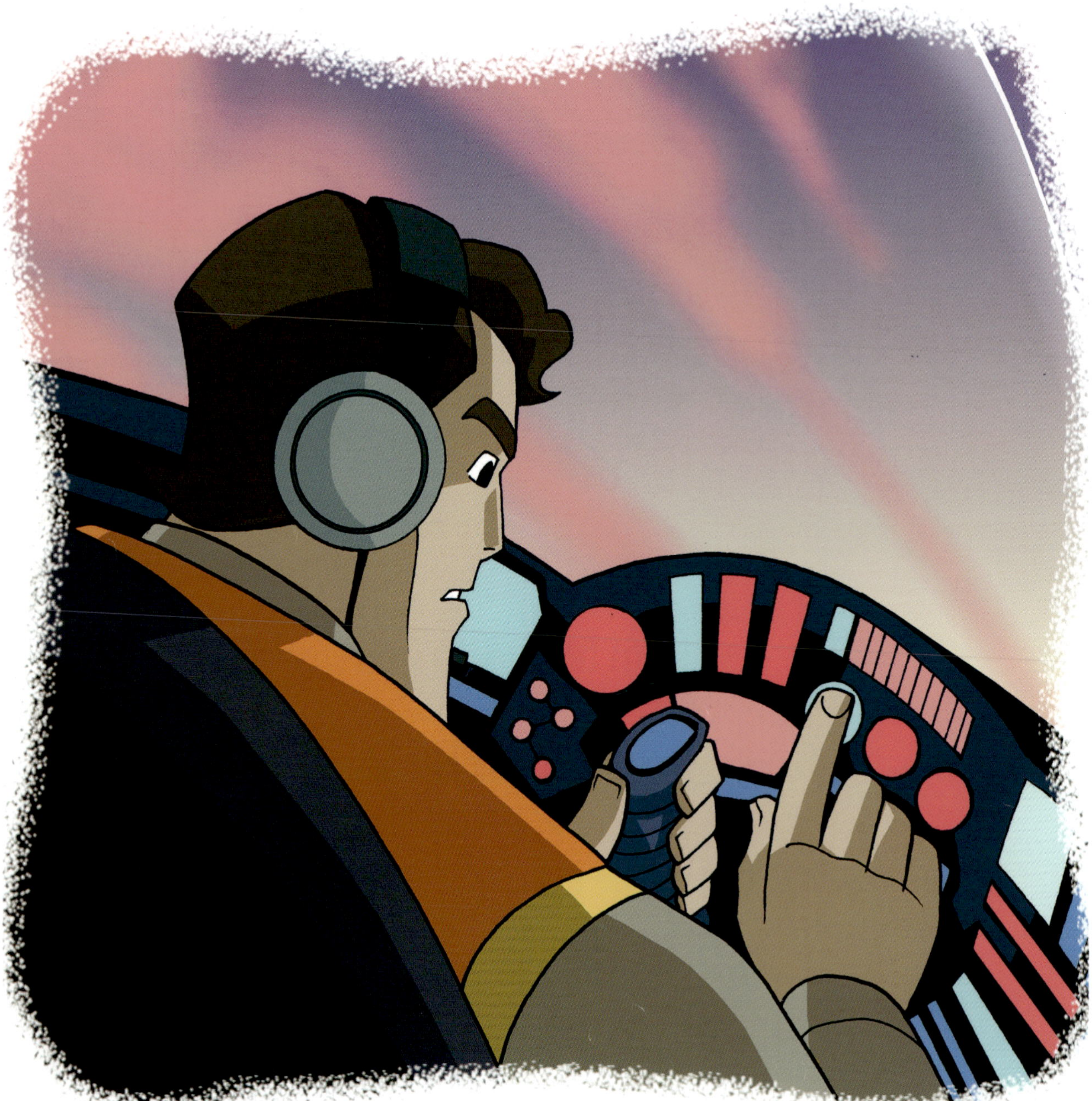

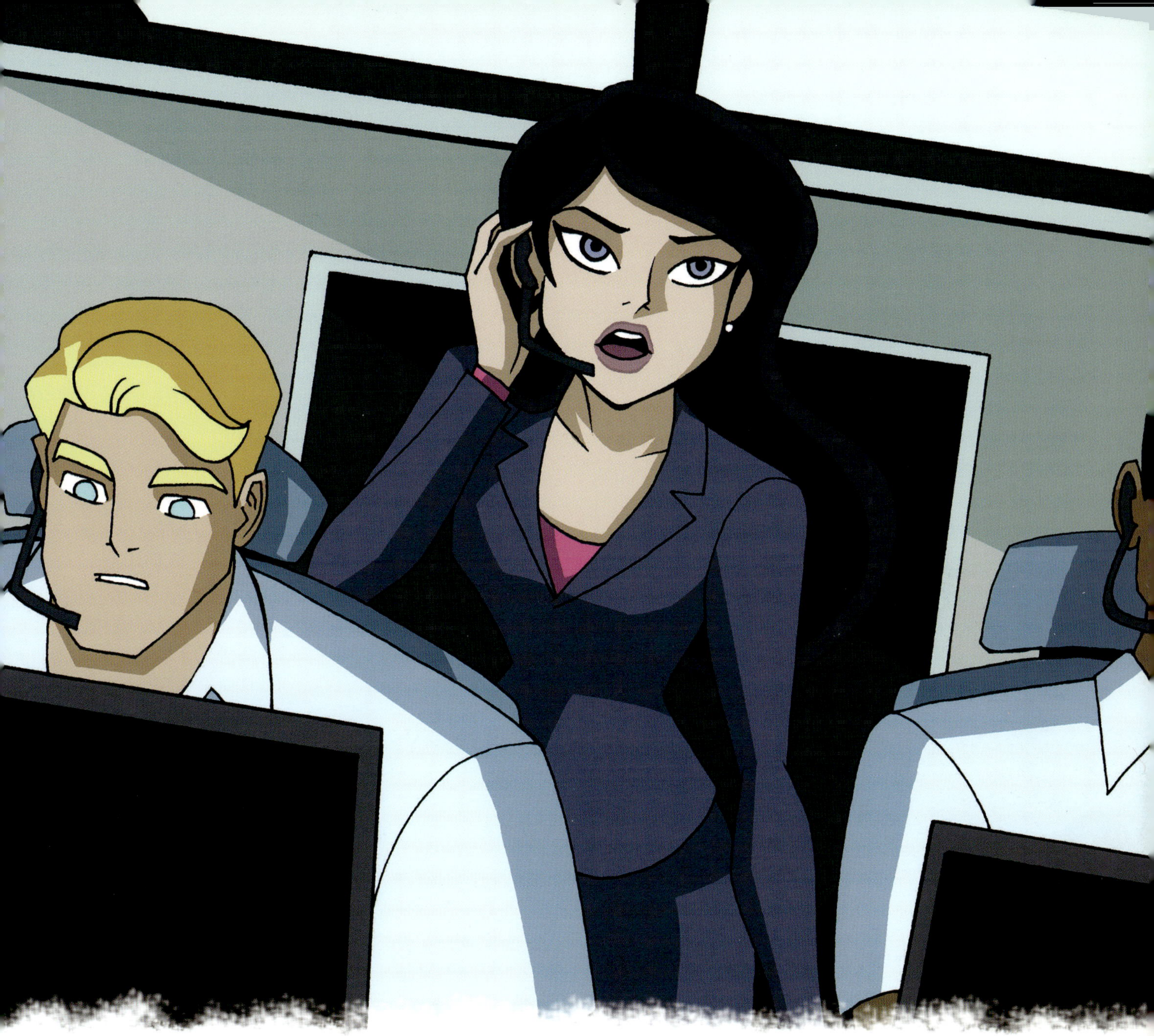

Carol's radio goes silent. "Hal?" Carol yells into her headset. "Hal, answer me!" But it's silent on the other end.

Hal pulls at the controls. They don't respond. He only has a few seconds to eject before the plane crashes.

Suddenly, everything starts to glow. A bright, emerald light floods the cockpit.

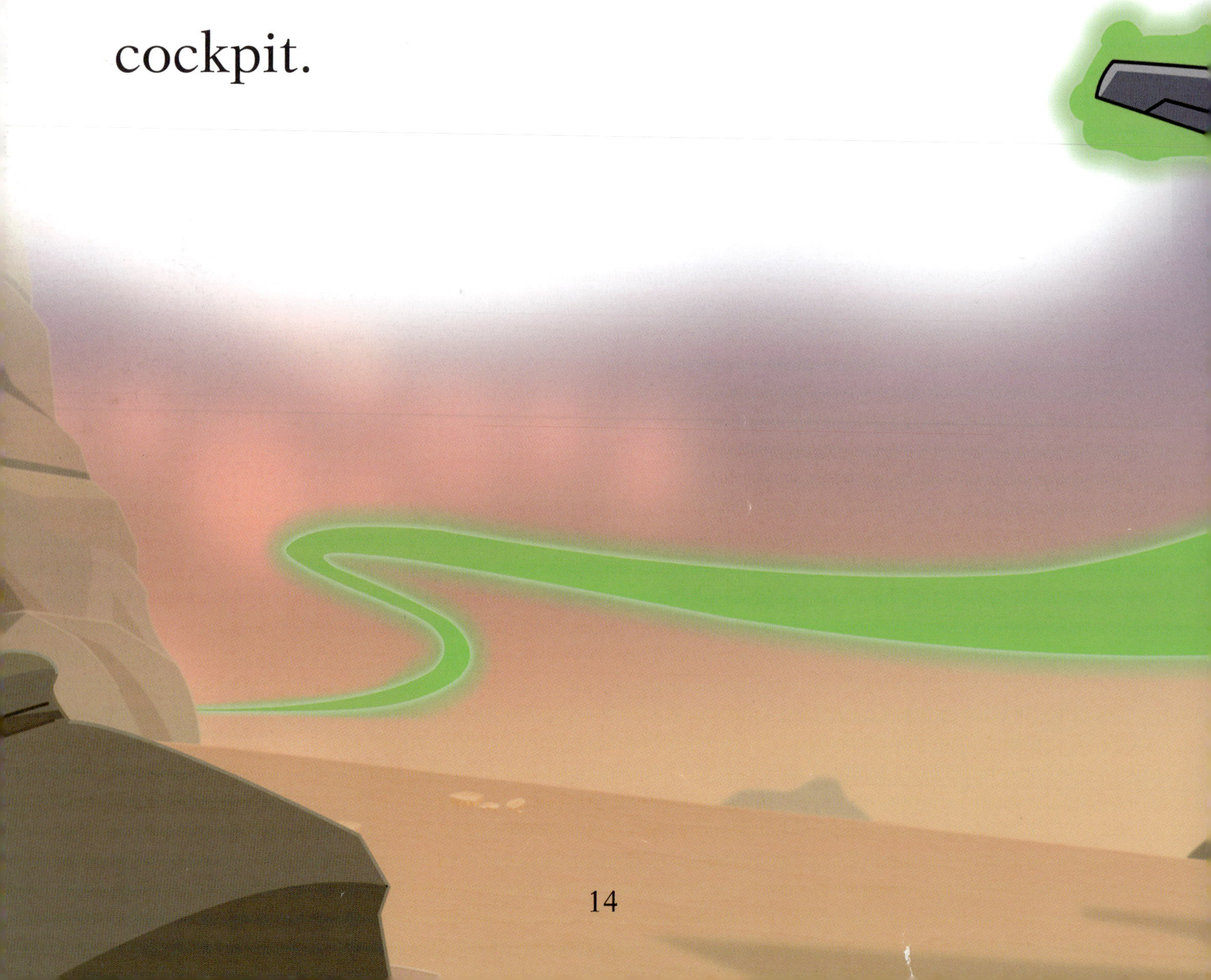

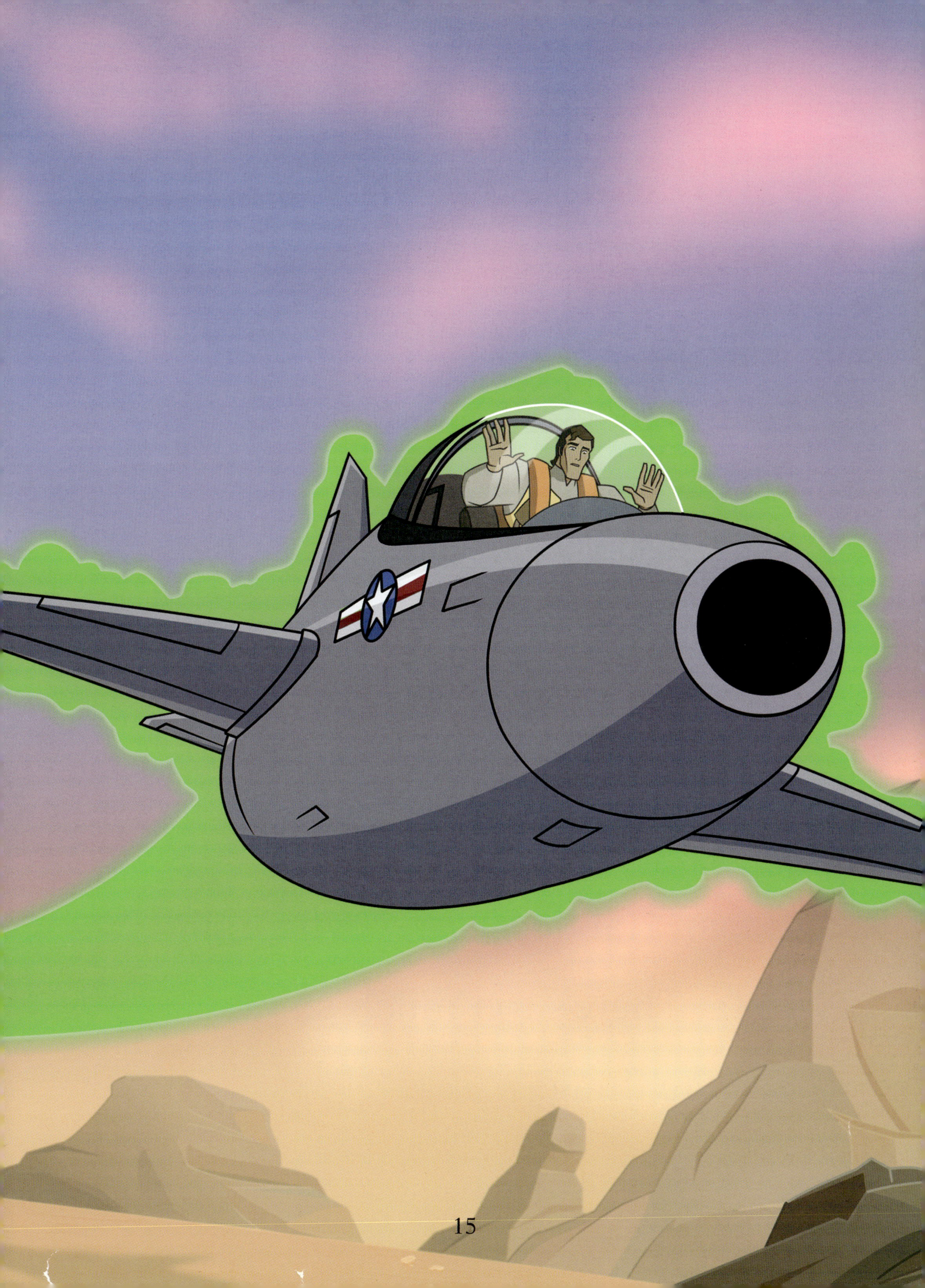

It takes thirty seconds for Hal's eyes to adjust. He can see again. But it takes him much longer to believe his eyes.

His plane is no longer falling. It's flying, lifted up by a strange green light.

The light finally sets the plane down. Hal doesn't recognize the area. There's too much smoke to see anything.

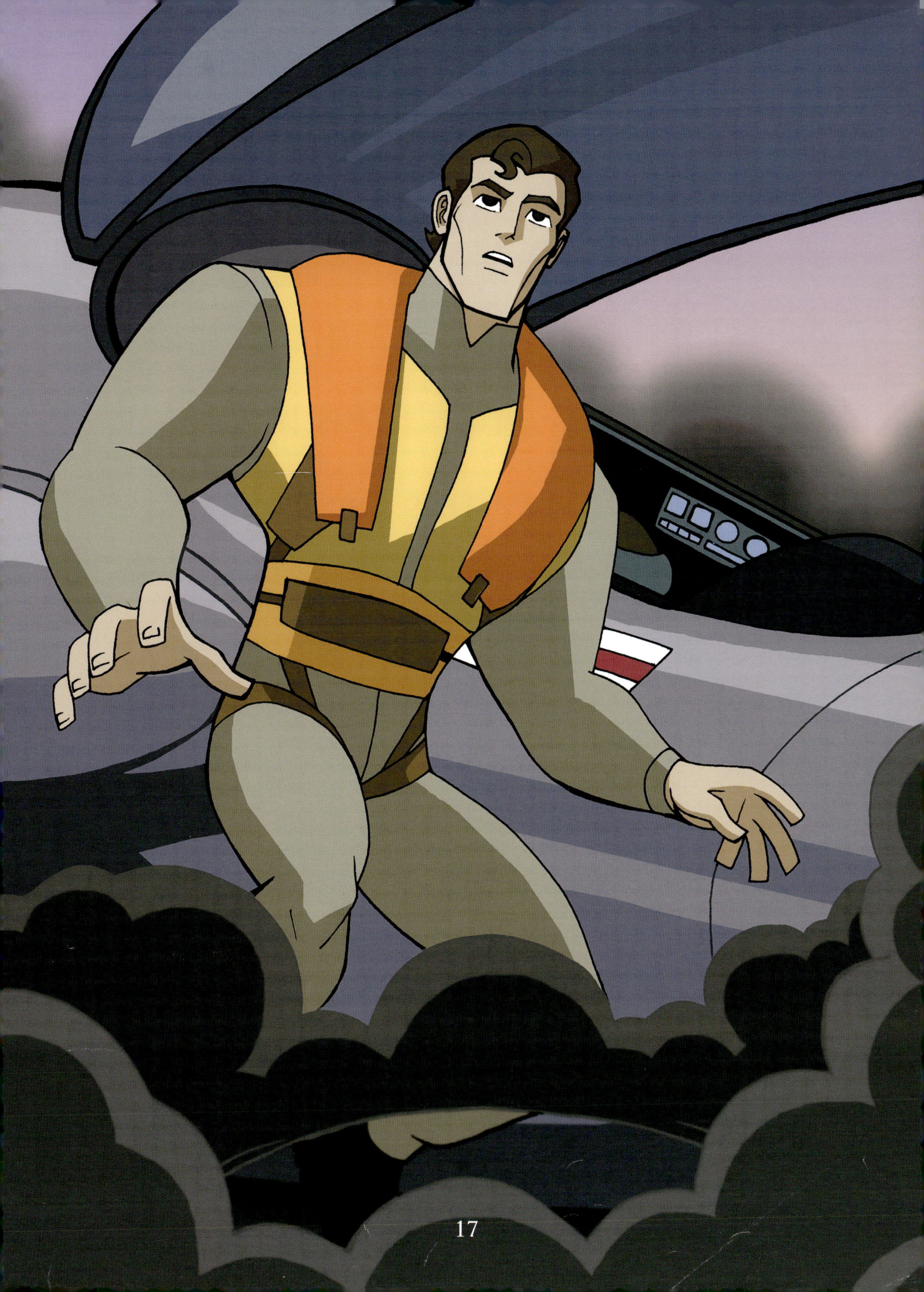

Then a green beam of light cuts through the smoke.

Hal follows the beam through the smoke. The craft on the other end of the light is waiting for him. Its bay door lowers.

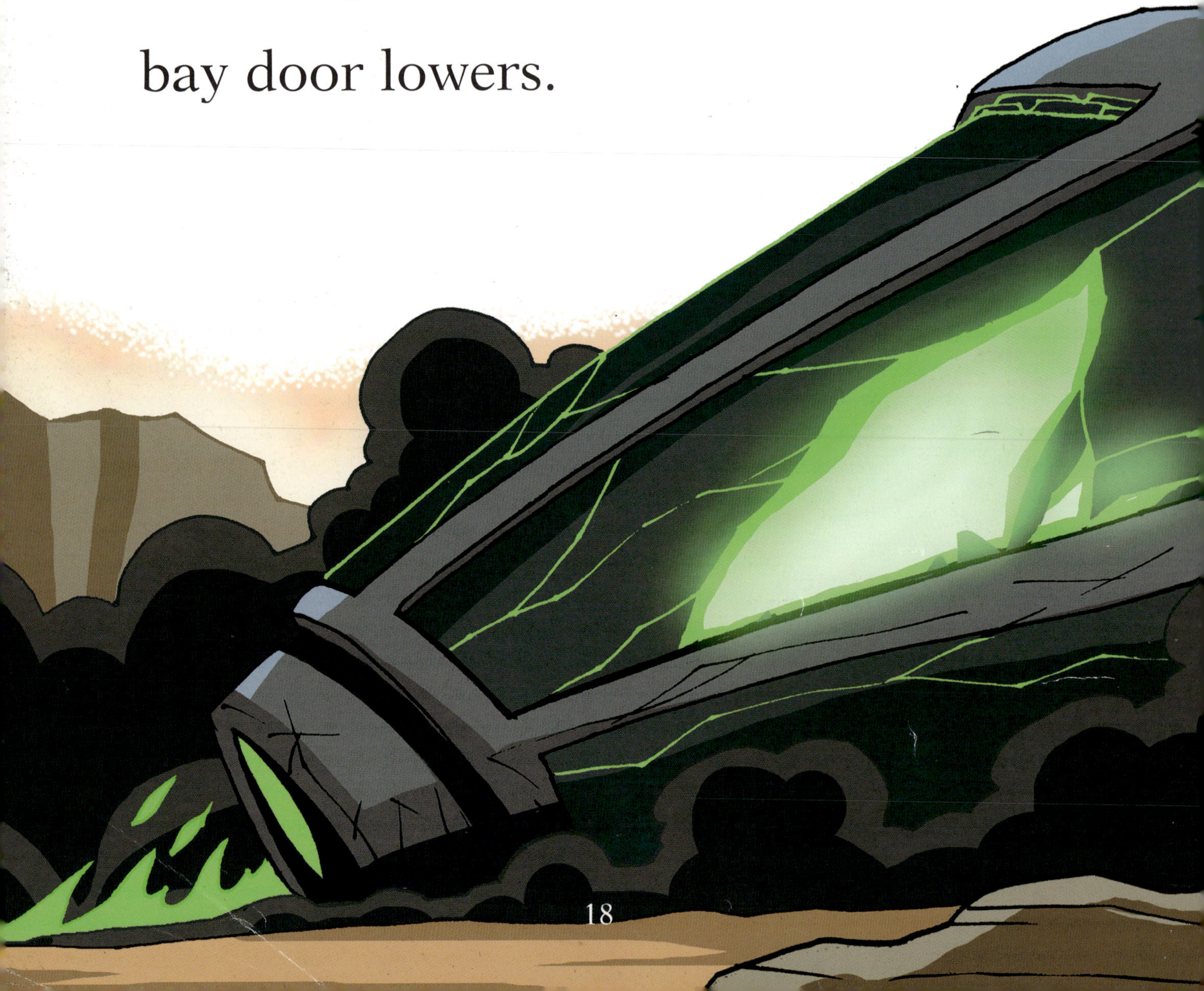

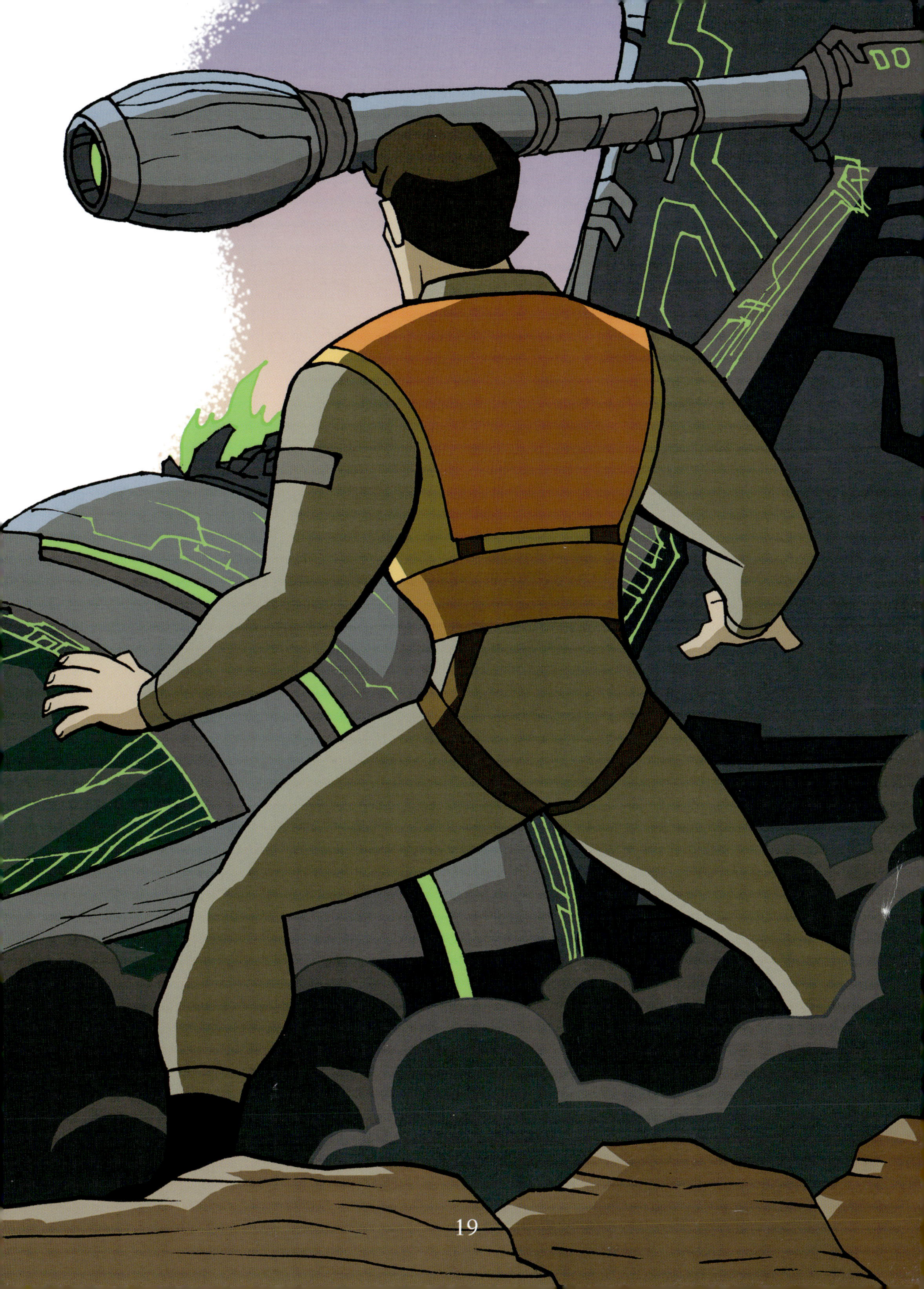

Abin Sur speaks. It is in a language Hal has never heard.

The ring on Abin Sur's finger translates for him. "Greetings," the ring says. "You must be the one I'm looking for."

Hal isn't sure what to say. So he says nothing. "You are not . . . running away at the sight of me," Abin Sur says. "That tells me the ring has chosen correctly. Your bravery and . . ."

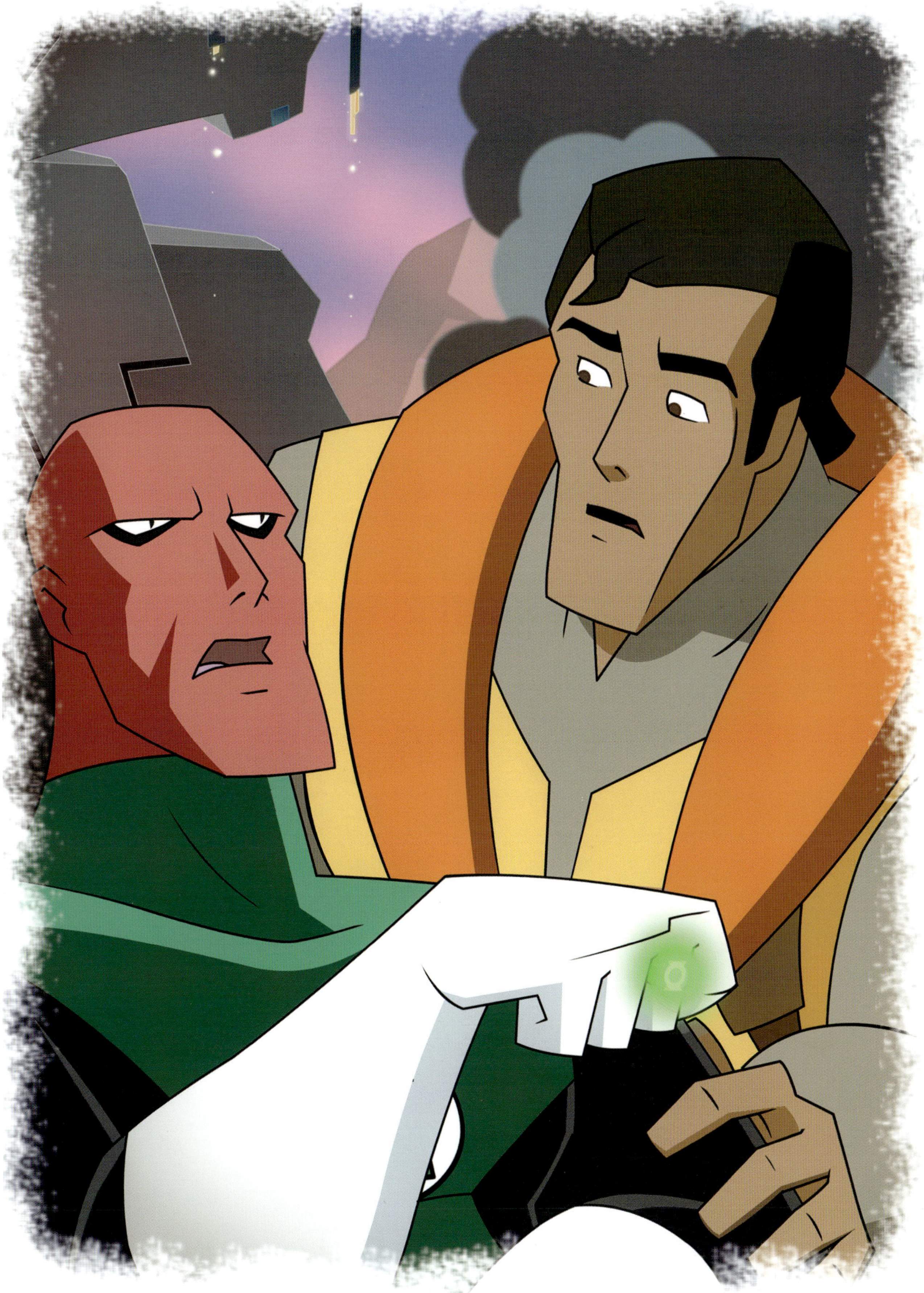

But the alien is too weak to say any more. He simply hands Hal Jordan his ring.

The ring touches Hal's fingers.

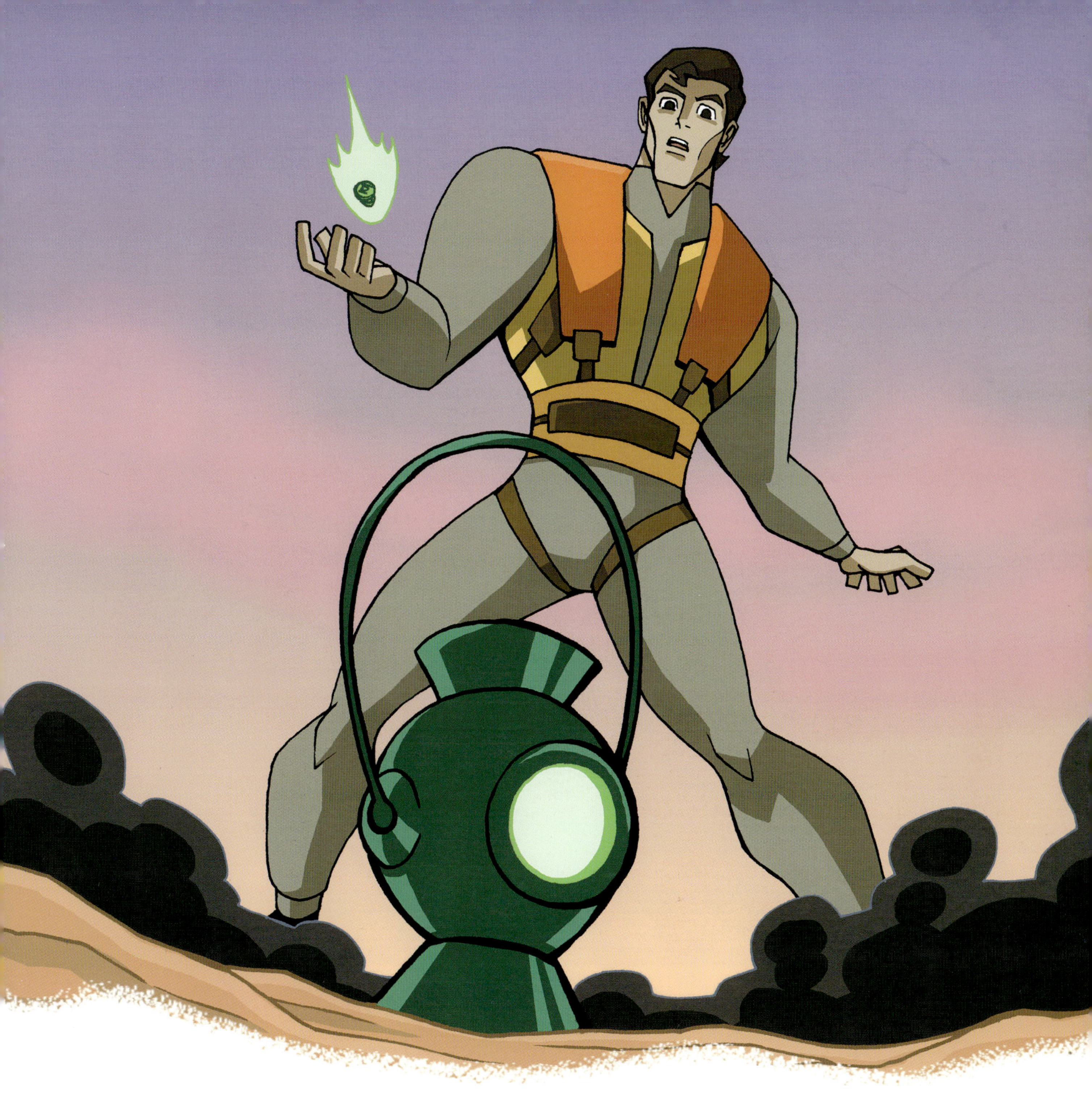

Abin Sur disappears. And so does the ship, fire, and smoke. All that's left is Hal and a glowing green lantern.

Hal pauses. Then he slips the ring on his own finger.

Hal takes a step back. Visions fill his mind. Beings in uniforms fly through the sky. They are on some distant world.

Somehow, Hal knows them — even though he has never seen them before.

They are defenders and heroes.

The vision ends. Hal looks down. He sees that he's wearing that same, strange uniform. He has become one of them.

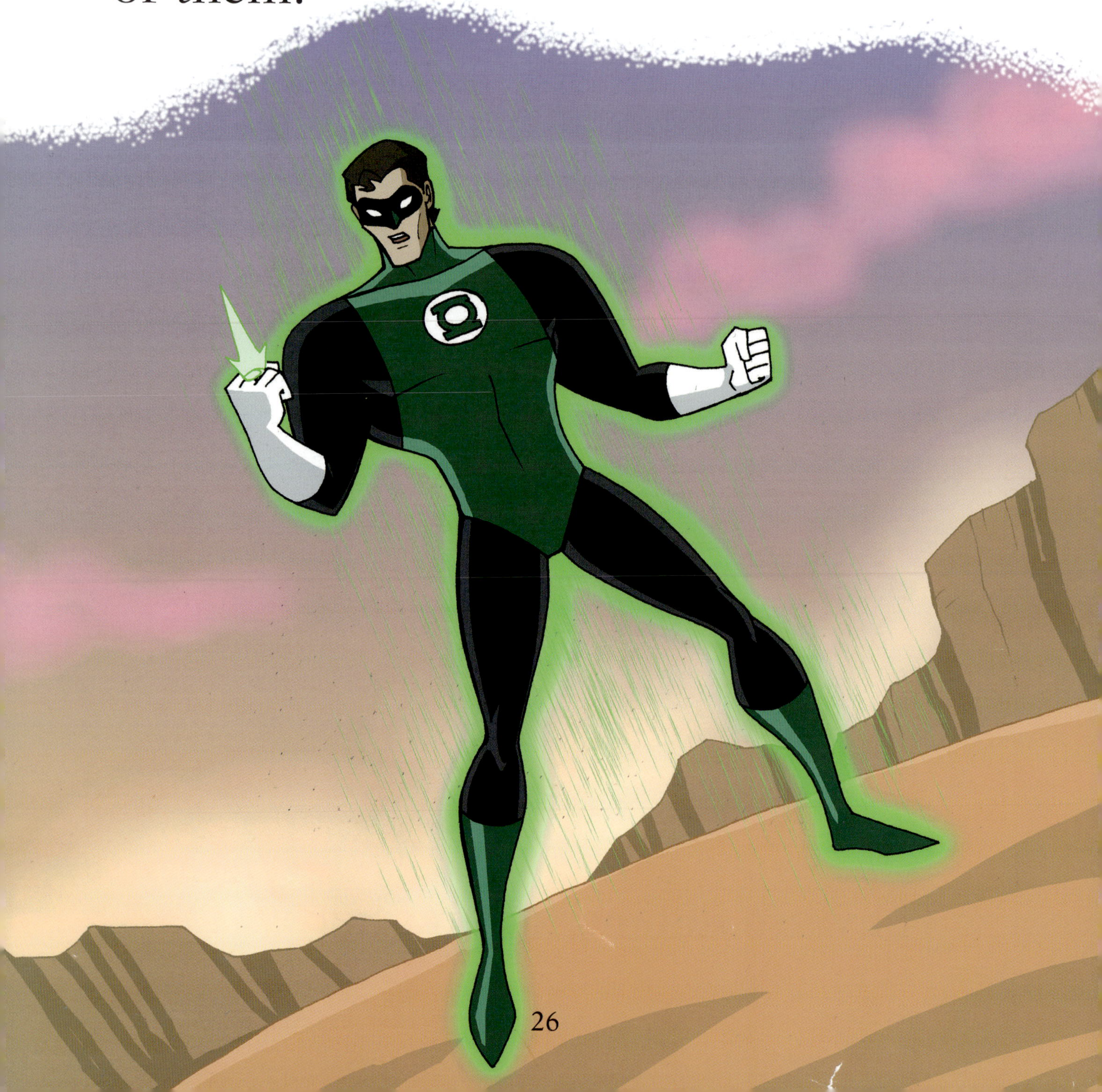

Carol's voice crackles from the jet's radio. "Hal?" she says. "Can you hear me? Are you there?"

"Great," Hal says under his breath. "How am I gonna get this thing airborne again?"

Then a bolt of green bursts from Hal's ring. It surrounds the jet. It rises into the air.

"Oh," he says. "I guess that'll work."

Hal takes a deep breath. He smiles. Then he concentrates and bends his knees. He jumps into the air.

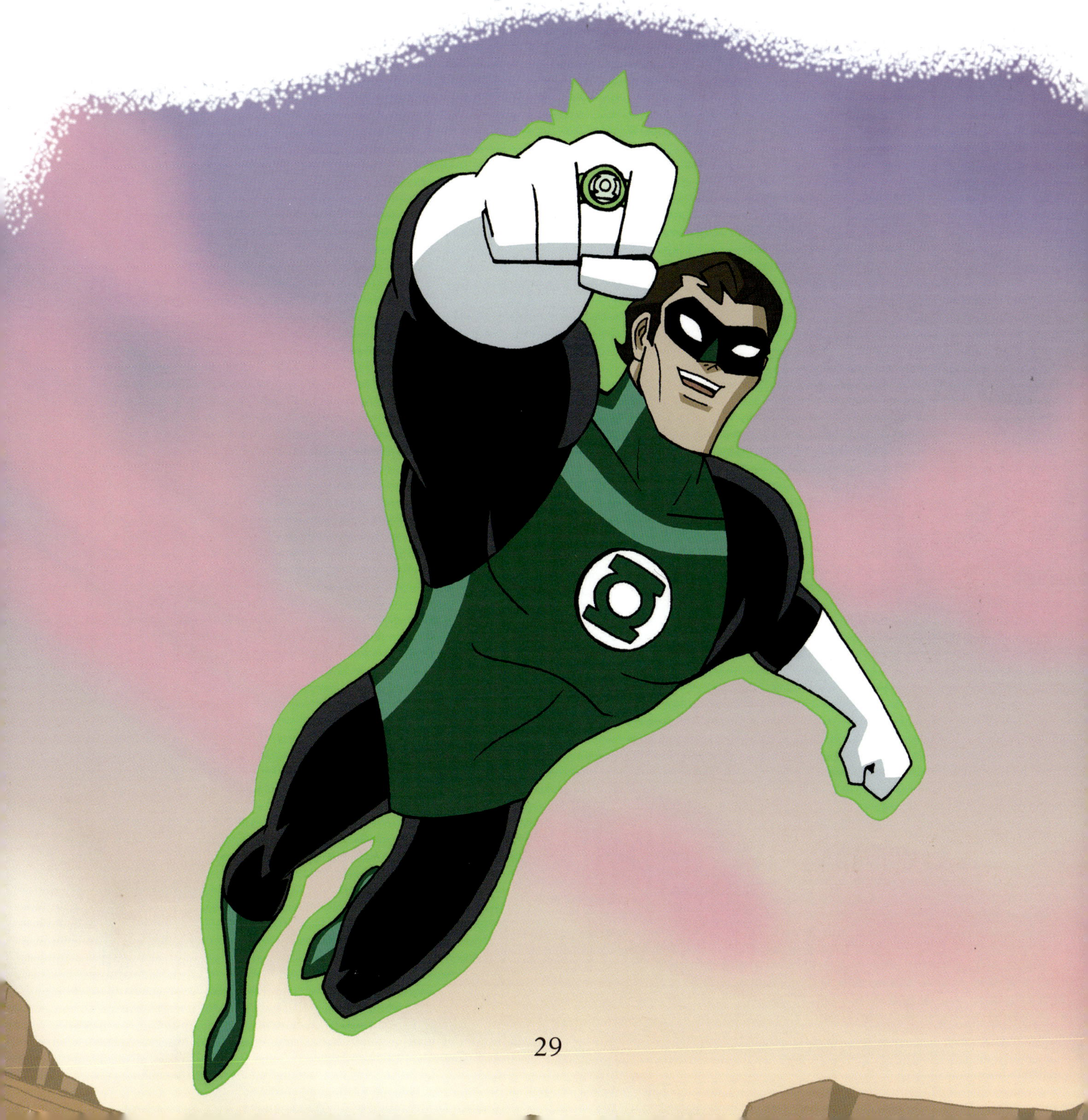

And just keeps on going.

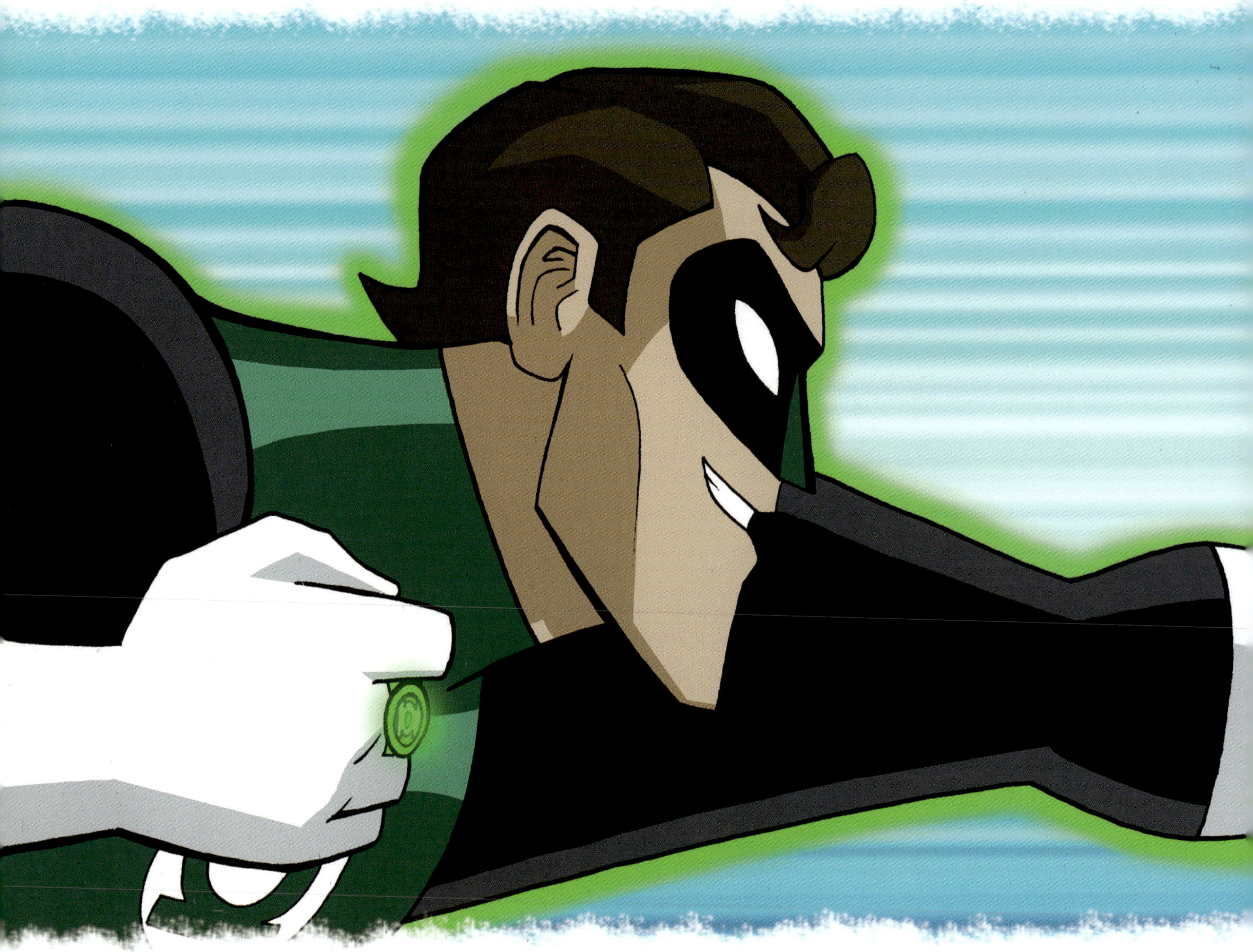

The jet follows him like an eager puppy on a leash. Hal smiles. This is a whole new kind of flying.

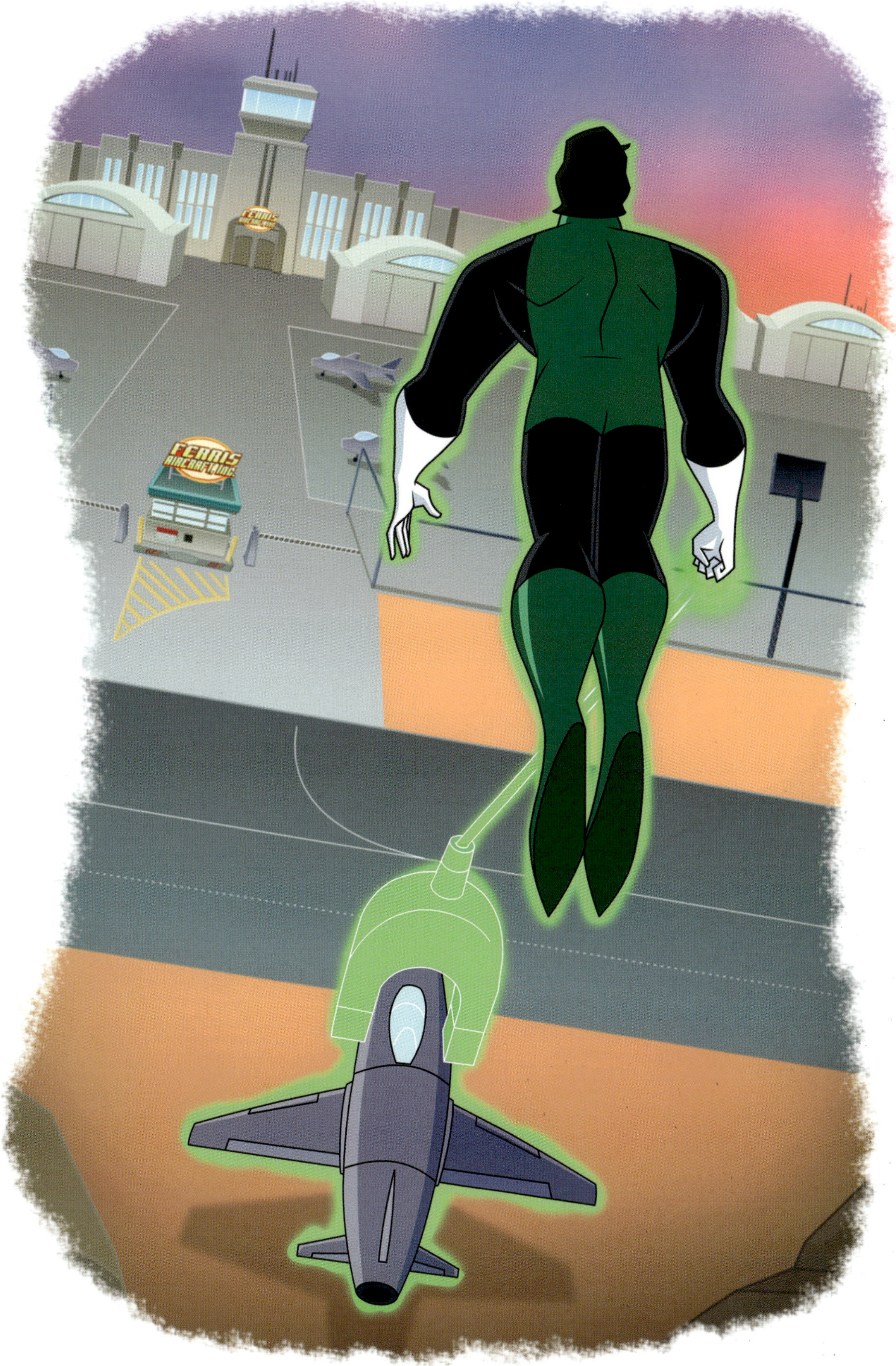
FERRIS AIRCRAFT INC.
FERRIS AIRCRAFT INC.

Soon Hal is back at Ferris Aircraft. He calmly walks to the control tower.

"Hal!" Carol cries. "How did you —?"

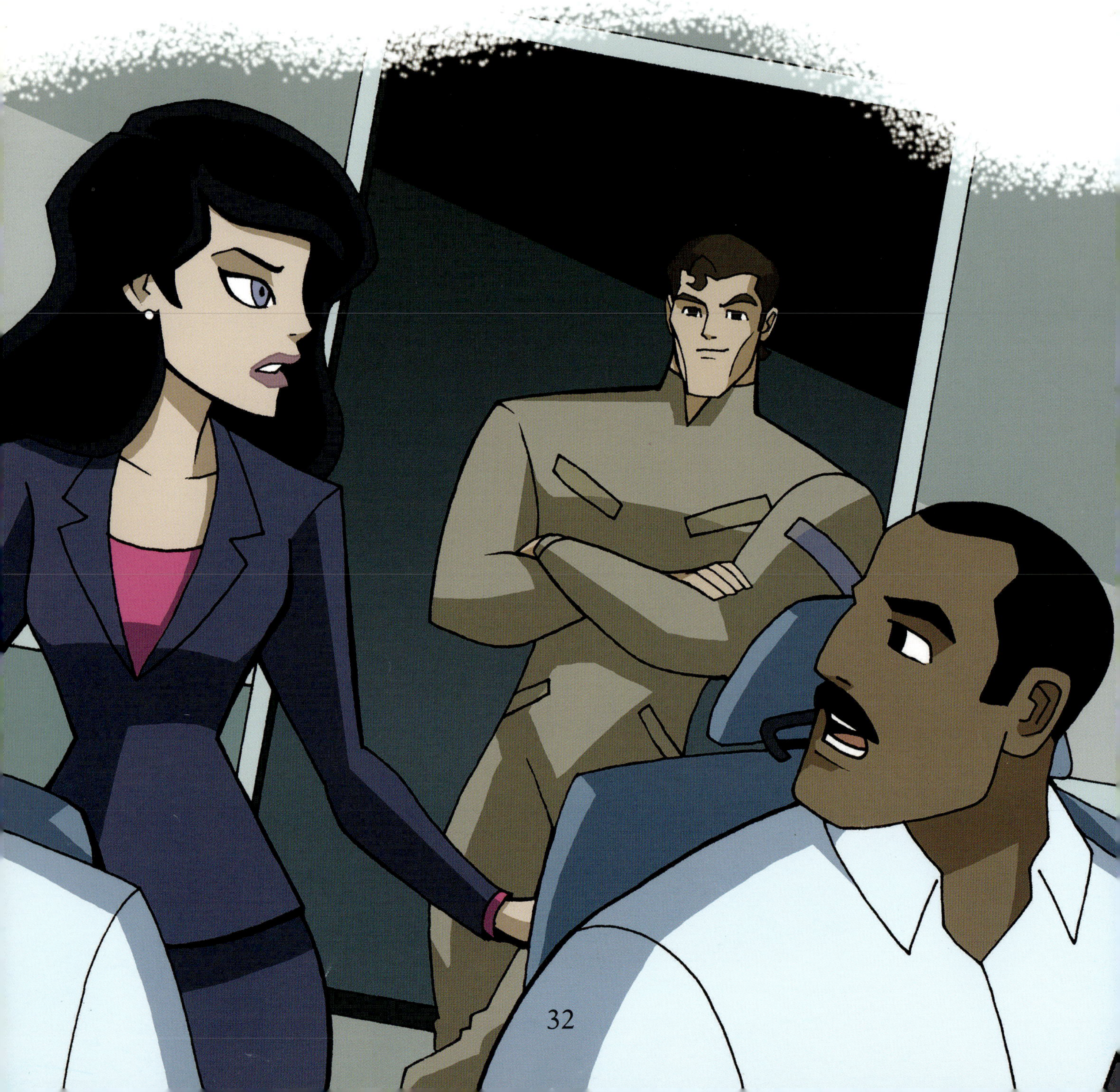

But the explanation will have
to wait. Another plane has lost
power. It's going down quickly. The
alien radiation from Abin Sur's
damaged ship still hangs in the air.
It is interfering with the plane's
equipment.

With all eyes on the sky, Hal heads to the locker room. He touches his ring to his lantern to charge it.

The ring sparks with energy.

Like a bolt of lightning, Hal shoots into the sky. He grits his teeth. He aims his ring.

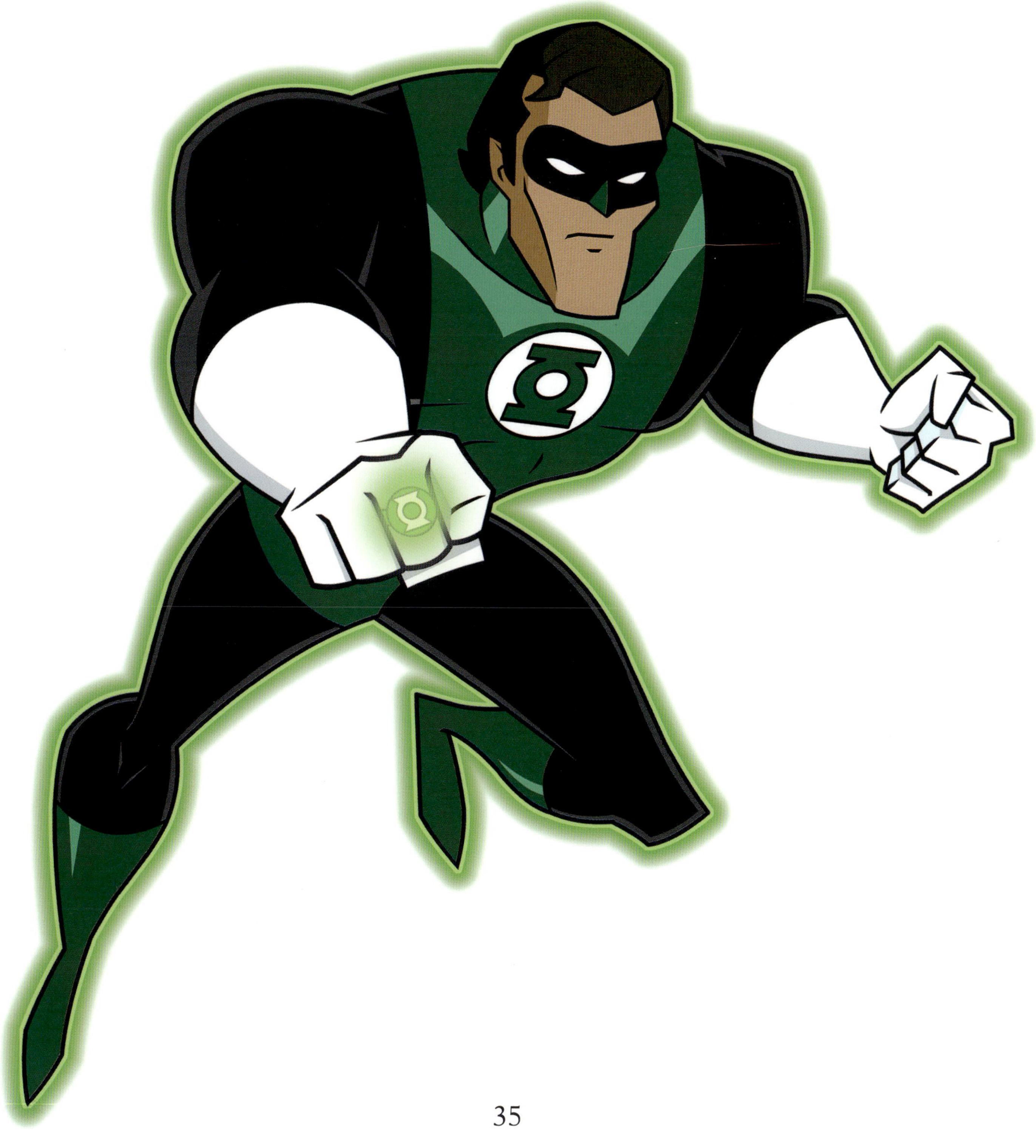

The ring hums. Energy surrounds the falling plane. Hal closes his eyes. He concentrates.

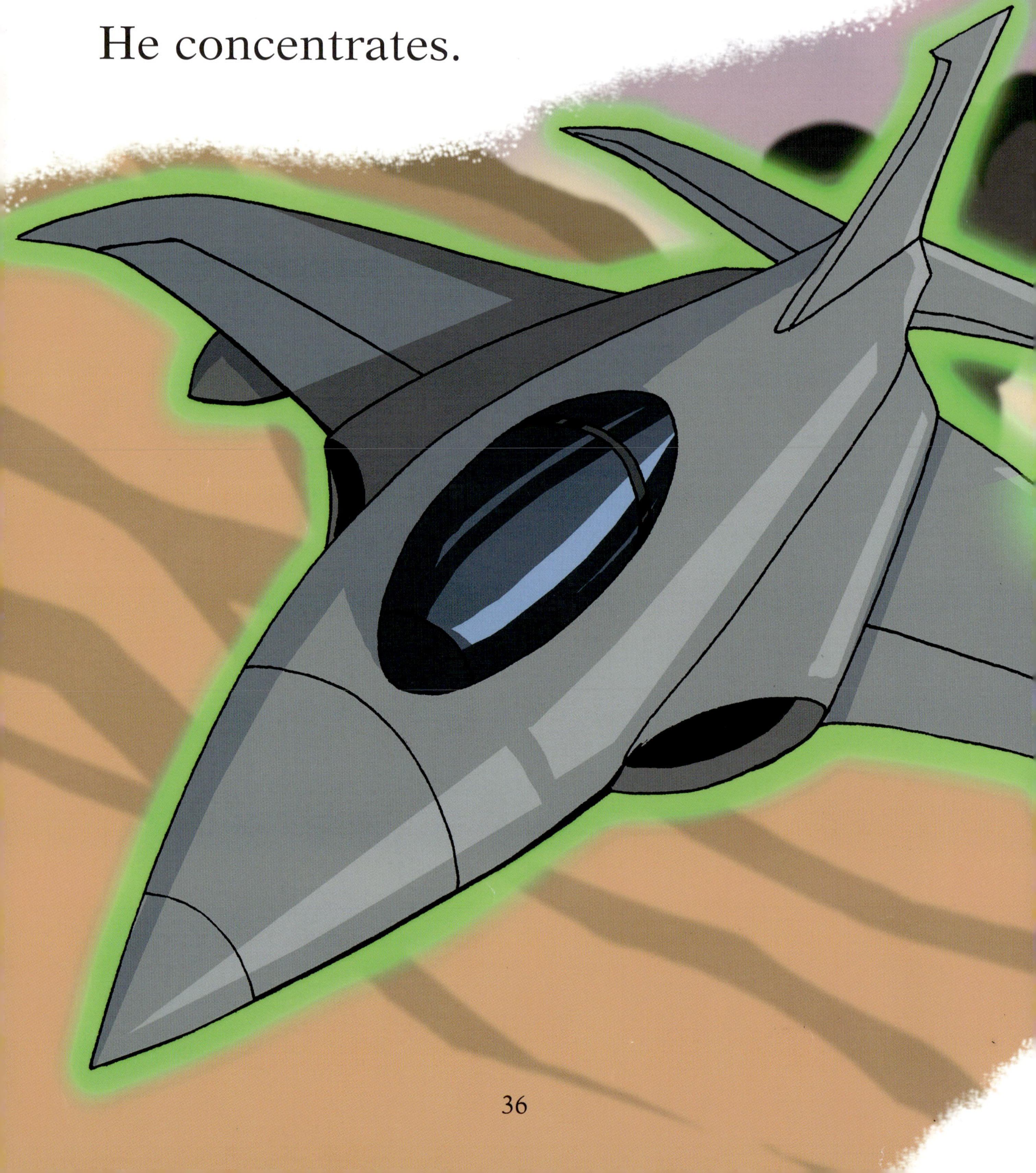

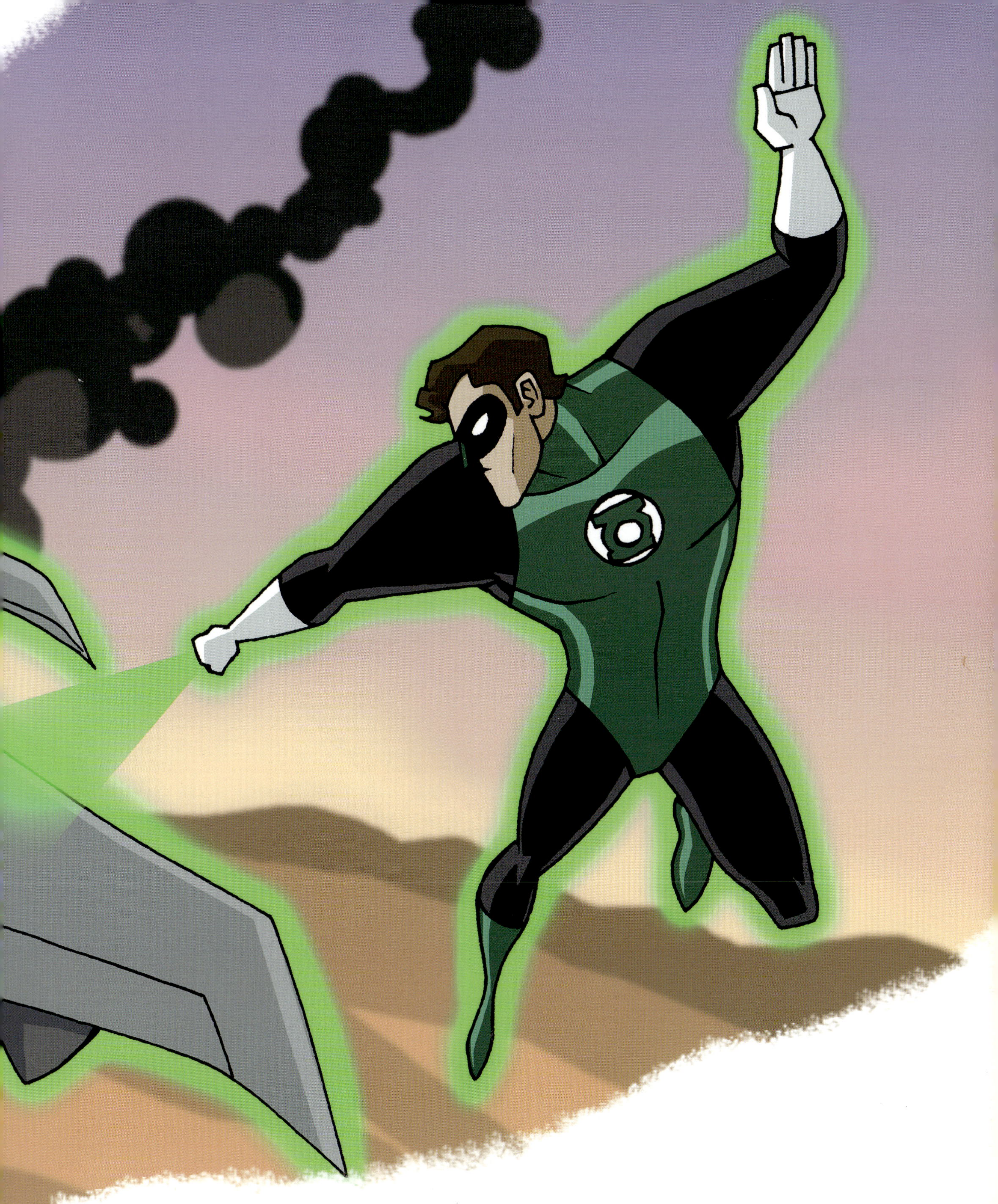

Hal gently sets the plane down.

"Wait!" Carol calls after him. "Who are you? How did you do that?!"

For once in his life, Hal Jordan stays quiet. He just smiles at Carol. Then he turns and flies away.

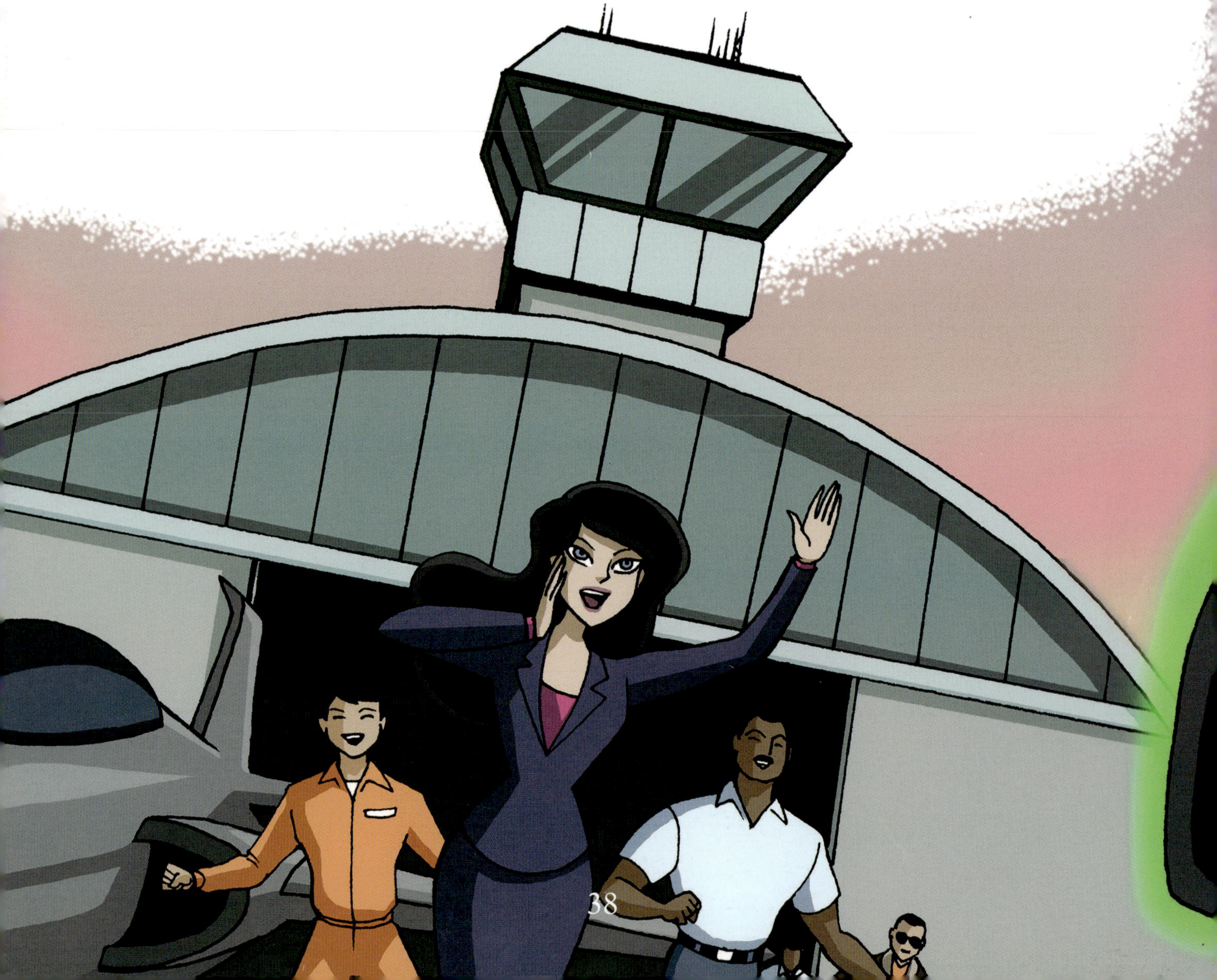

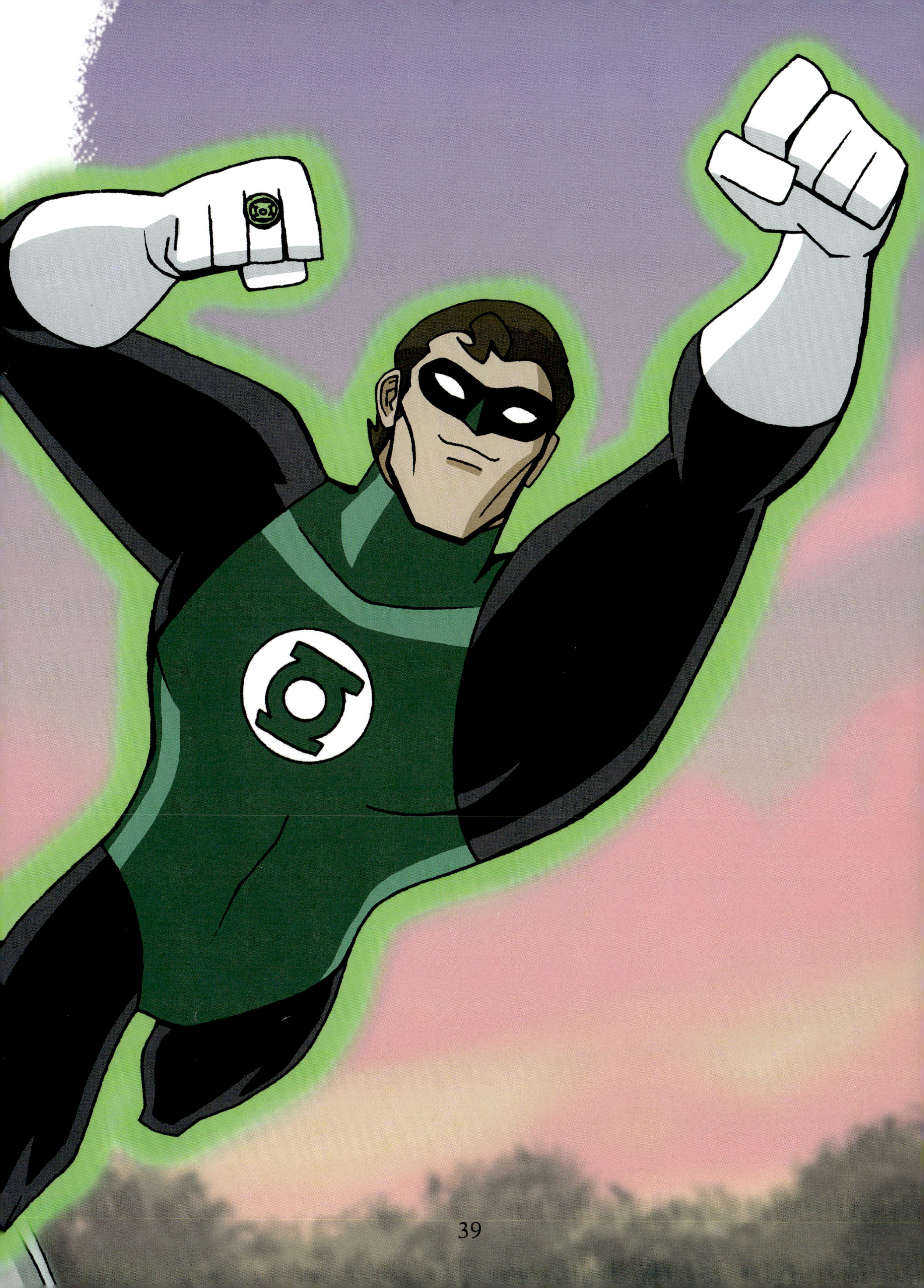

Hal travels to a distant planet called Oa. There he will learn his super hero mission. And he will learn the Green Lantern's oath . . .

"In brightest day, in blackest night, no evil shall escape my sight. Let those who worship evil's might, beware my power . . . Green Lantern's light!"

Hal will use his willpower to defeat his fears. He will protect the beings of Sector 2814 against all evils. He is the greatest Green Lantern!

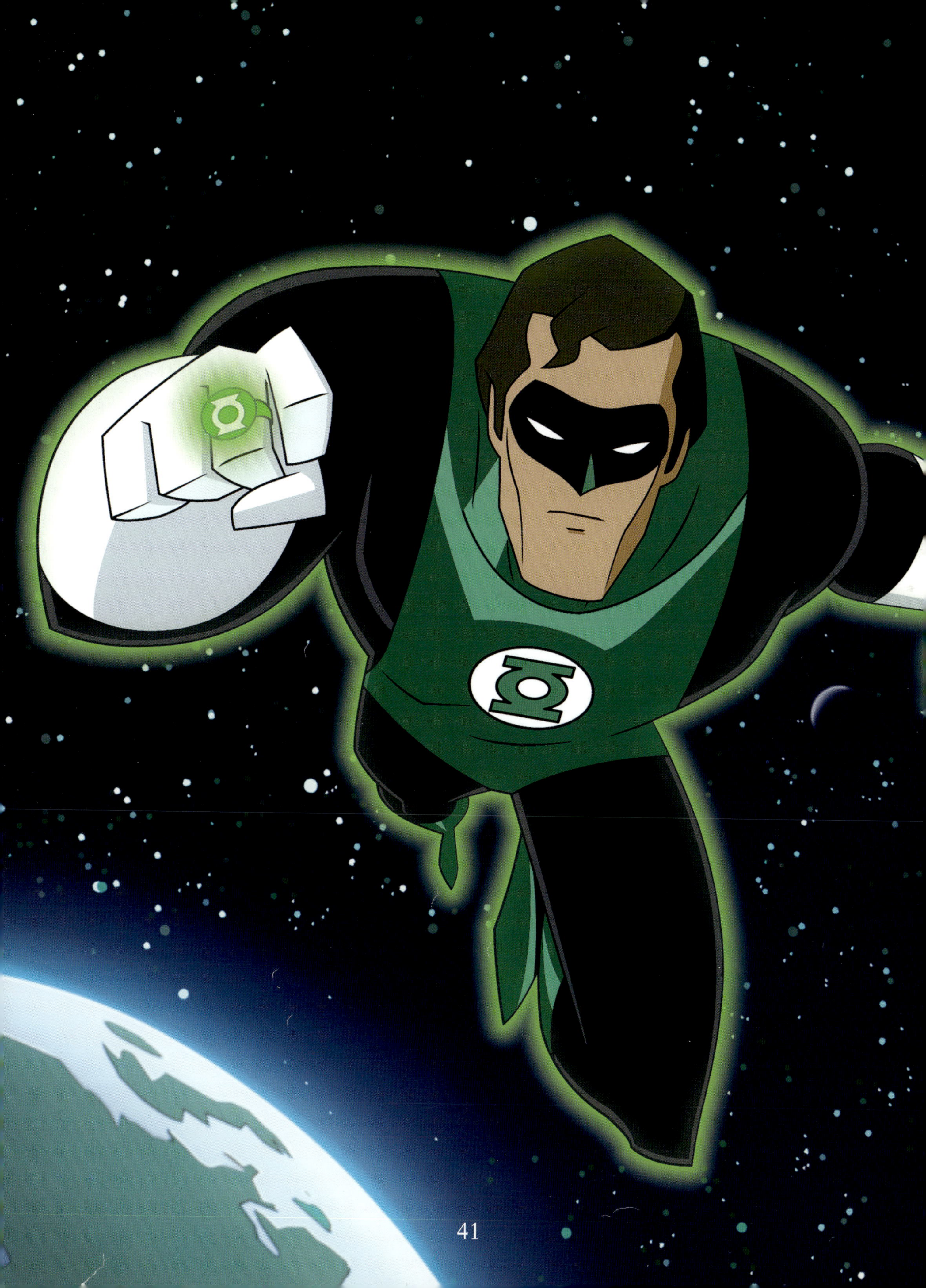

EVERYTHING ABOUT...

GREEN LANTERN™

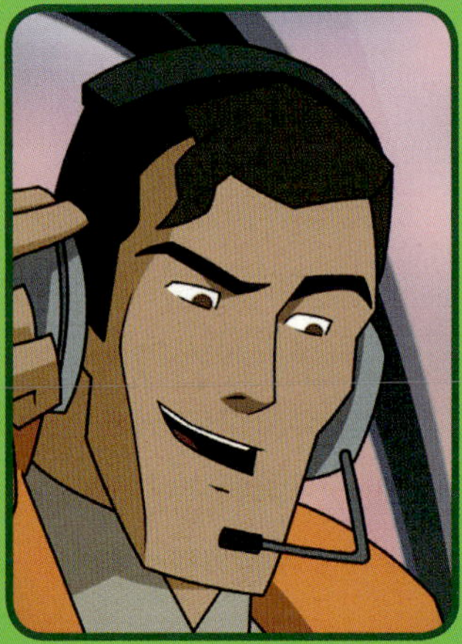

REAL NAME: HAL JORDAN

ROLE: INTERGALACTIC GUARDIAN

BASE: SECTOR 2814

A former test pilot, Hal Jordan has learned to remain calm under pressure. But it takes every ounce of willpower he has to be the greatest Green Lantern!

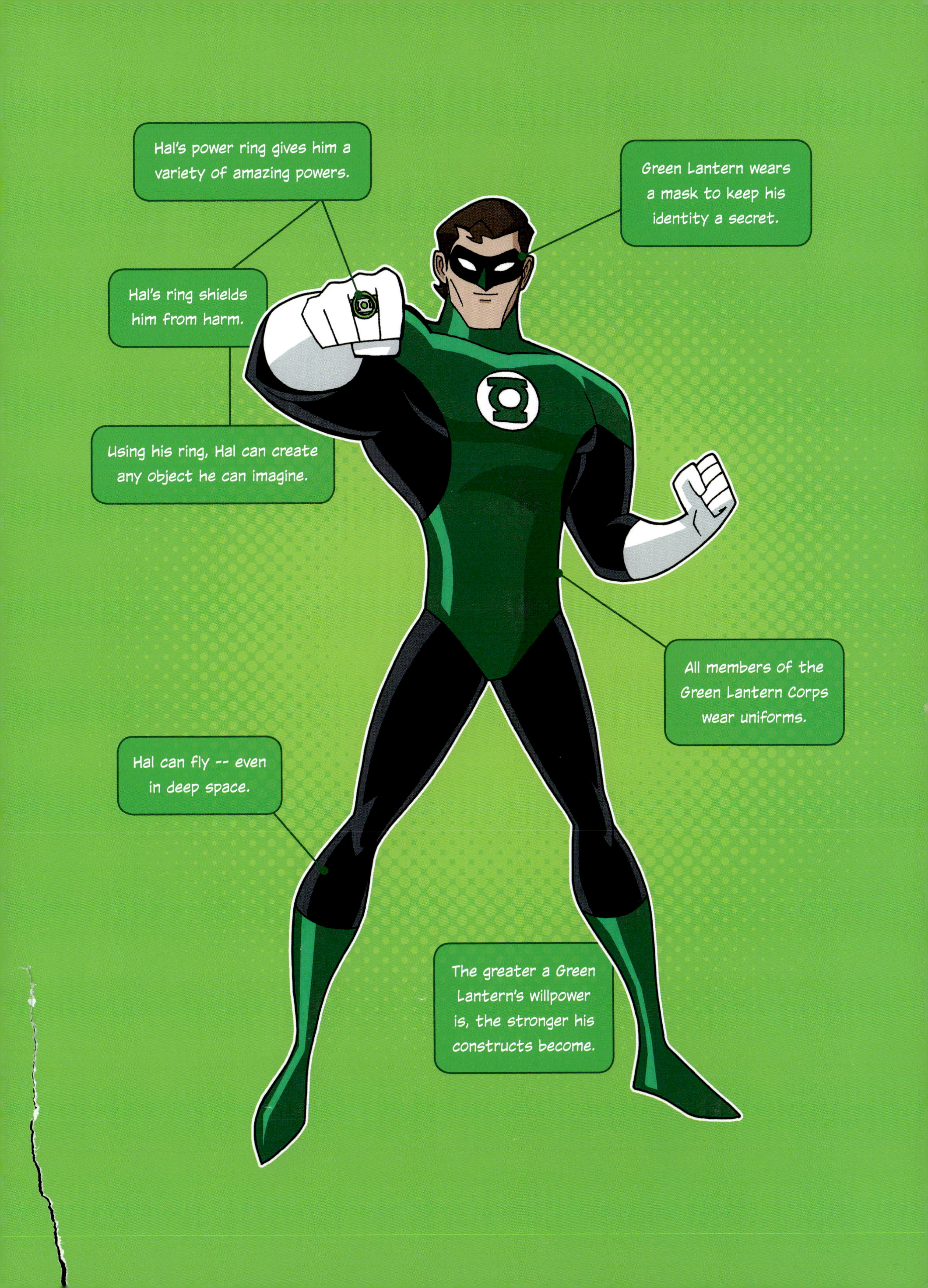
Hal's power ring gives him a variety of amazing powers.
Green Lantern wears a mask to keep his identity a secret.
Hal's ring shields him from harm.
Using his ring, Hal can create any object he can imagine.
All members of the Green Lantern Corps wear uniforms.
Hal can fly -- even in deep space.
The greater a Green Lantern's willpower is, the stronger his constructs become.

THE AUTHOR

Over the course of **MATTHEW K. MANNING**'s writing career, he has written comics or books starring Batman, Superman, the Flash, the Justice League, and even Bugs Bunny. Some of his more recent works include the popular hardcover for Andrews McMeel Publishing entitled *The Batman Files*, a graphic novel retelling of *The Fall of the House of Usher*, and several DC Super Heroes books for Stone Arch Books. He lives in Mystic, Connecticut with his wife Dorothy and daughter Lillian.

THE ILLUSTRATOR

LUCIANO VECCHIO was born in 1982 and currently lives in Buenos Aires, Argentina. With experience in illustration, animation, and comics, his works have been published in the US, Spain, UK, France, and Argentina. His credits include Ben 10 (DC Comics), Cruel Thing (Norma), Unseen Tribe (Zuda Comics), and Sentinels (Drumfish Productions).

GLOSSARY

atmosphere (AT-muhss-feer)—the various gases that surround a planet or star

champion (CHAM-pee-uhn)—someone who fights or speaks publicly in support of something

concentrates (CON-suhn-trayts)—thinks about something or focuses on something specific

deafening (DEFF-uh-ning)—extremely loud

interfering (in-ter-FEER-ing)—stopping, slowing, or preventing someone or something

plummets (PLUHM-itz)—falls suddenly straight down (usually from a very high place)

radiation (ray-dee-A-shuhn)—energy that comes from a source in the form of waves or rays you cannot see. Radiation is often harmful.

recognize (REK-uhg-nize)—to know or remember someone or something because of previous knowledge or experience

willpower (WILL-pow-er)—the strong determination that allows you to do something difficult, or the ability to control yourself

DISCUSSION QUESTIONS

Write down your answers. Refer back to the story for help.

QUESTION 1.

Hal flies through the air. We see lines in the background. Why are these lines present? What do they mean?

QUESTION 2.

Hal carries his aircraft back to base using a giant magnet. What are some other ways Hal could have used his power ring to bring the plane back?

QUESTION 3.

How did Abin Sur find Hal? Why did he choose Hal to be his replacement?

QUESTION 4.

Where does this line of green energy lead? Who is creating it, and why? How do you know?

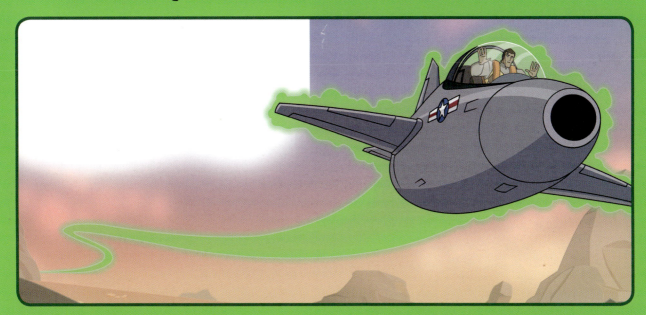

READ THEM ALL!!

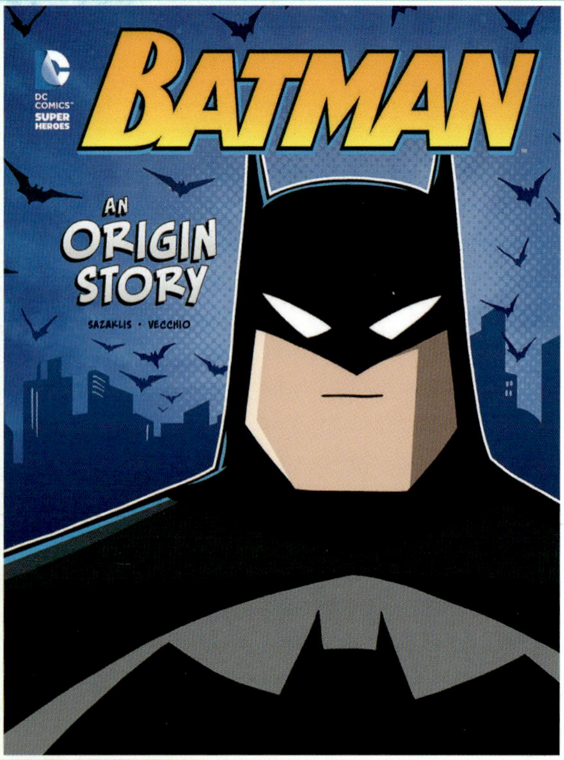
BATMAN
AN ORIGIN STORY
SAZAKLIS • VECCHIO

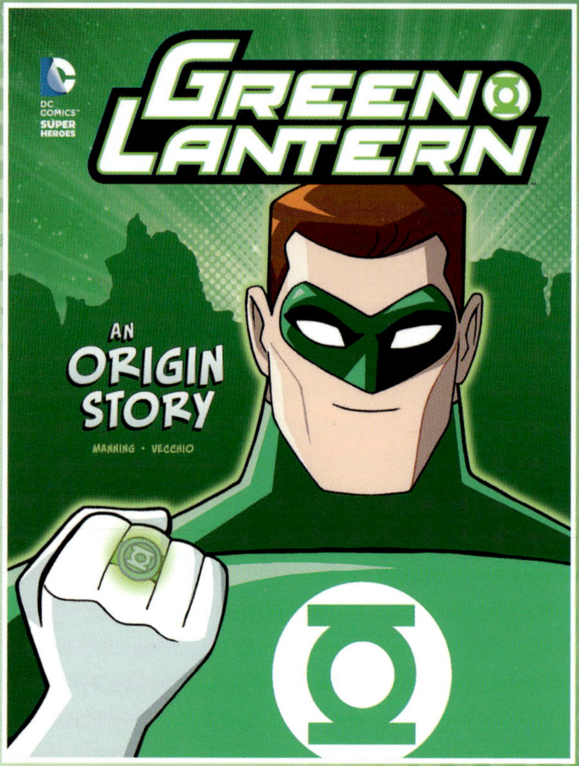
GREEN LANTERN
AN ORIGIN STORY
MANNING • VECCHIO

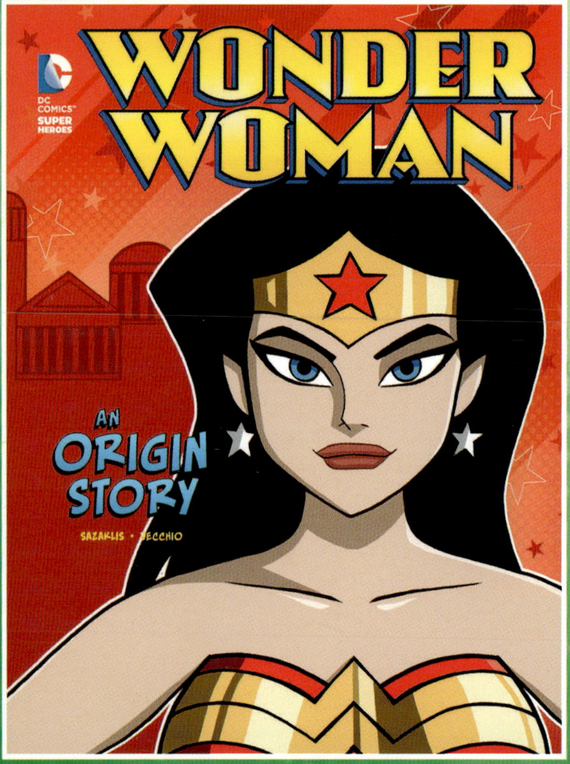
WONDER WOMAN
AN ORIGIN STORY
SAZAKLIS • VECCHIO

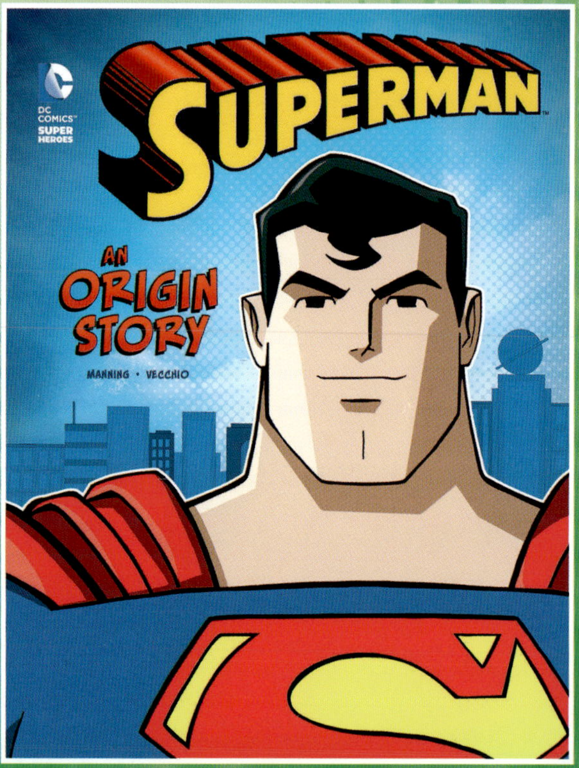
SUPERMAN
AN ORIGIN STORY
MANNING • VECCHIO

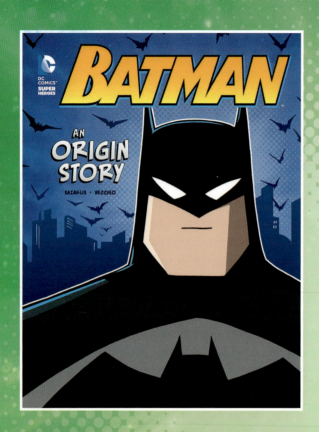